THE WHITE REVIEW

26

CELINE

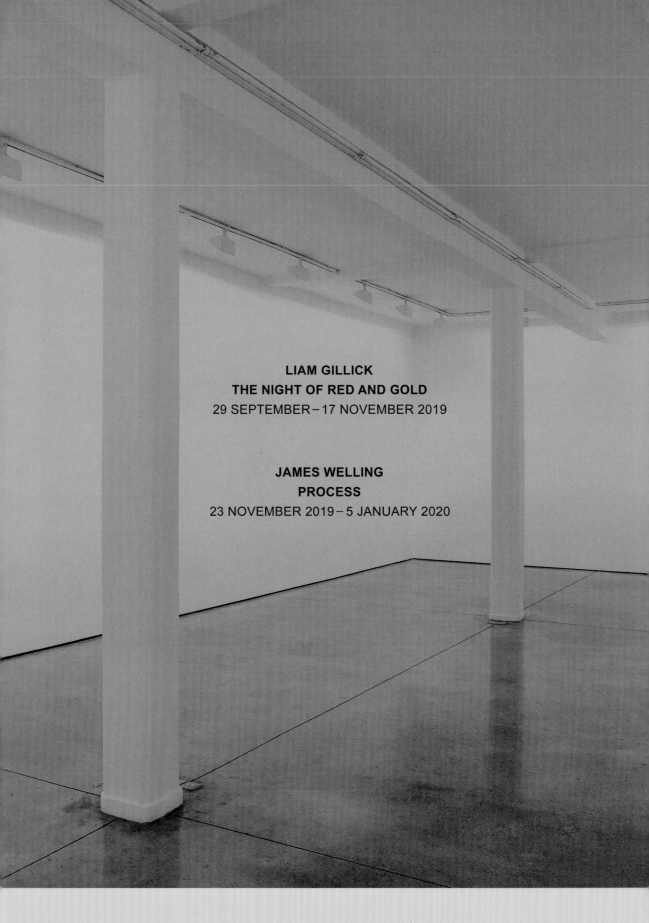

LIAM GILLICK
THE NIGHT OF RED AND GOLD
29 SEPTEMBER – 17 NOVEMBER 2019

JAMES WELLING
PROCESS
23 NOVEMBER 2019 – 5 JANUARY 2020

MAUREEN PALEY.   21 HERALD STREET, LONDON E2 6JT   T: +44 (0)20 7729 4112   MAUREENPALEY.COM

HAUSER & WIRTH PUBLISHERS

SINCE 1992

2019 NEW RELEASES

WWW.HAUSERWIRTH.COM/PUBLISHERS

PHOTO: ED PARK

SOUTHBANK CENTRE

London Literature Festival

AND POETRY INTERNATIONAL

ONCE UPON OUR TIMES

NIKKI GIOVANNI   LEMN SISSAY   ANTHONY DANIELS

HEATHER MORRIS   JUNG CHANG   BRETT ANDERSON

17 - 27 OCT

LOTTERY FUNDED

Supported using public funding by
ARTS COUNCIL
ENGLAND

TACTILE CHANGE

AN EXHIBITION
by Matthew Raw
of contemporary ceramics
questioning our response
to the challenges and everyday
rhetoric of societal progress

FROM 20 September
UNTIL 16 November 2019

THE GALLERY
at Plymouth College of Art
Tavistock Place, PL4 8AT
PLYMOUTHART.AC.UK/GALLERY

MON TO FRI (9am — 5pm)
SAT (10am — 1pm)

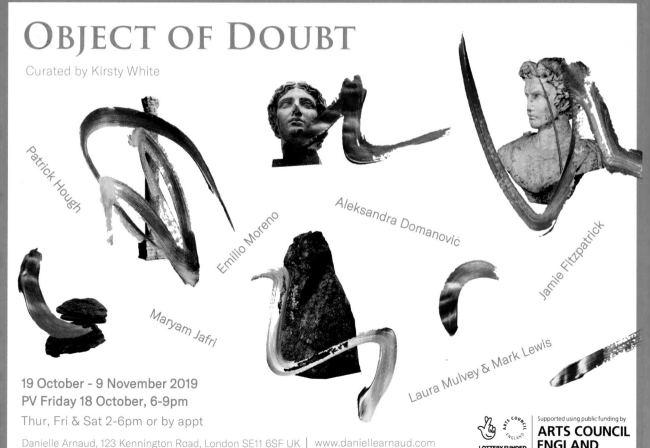

OBJECT OF DOUBT

Curated by Kirsty White

Patrick Hough

Emilio Moreno

Aleksandra Domanović

Jamie Fitzpatrick

Maryam Jafri

Laura Mulvey & Mark Lewis

19 October - 9 November 2019
PV Friday 18 October, 6-9pm

Thur, Fri & Sat 2-6pm or by appt

Danielle Arnaud, 123 Kennington Road, London SE11 6SF UK | www.daniellearnaud.com

Supported using public funding by
ARTS COUNCIL
ENGLAND

LOTTERY FUNDED

Published by The White Review, September 2019
Edition of 1,800

Printed by Unicum, Tilburg
Typeset in Nouveau Blanche

ISBN No. 978-0-9957437-8-6

The White Review is a registered charity (number 1148690)

The White Review, 8–12 Creekside, London SE8 3DX
www.thewhitereview.org

Supported using public funding by
ARTS COUNCIL ENGLAND
LOTTERY FUNDED

EDITORIAL

At the close of this issue's interview with Elad Lassry, who has also provided us with a new artwork for our cover, the artist considers the proposition that 'everything is art'. Lassry admits he finds this viewpoint challenging. 'Trees, deserts, oceans are phenomena,' he argues. 'Art is the decision.'

Many of the writers in issue 26 choose a decisive and critical position from which to work, challenging the political situations they see unfolding around them. An extract from Shumona Sinha's searing novel *Let's Knock Out the Poor* is a reckoning with France's treatment of migrants and asylum seekers based on the author's own experience of working in an immigration centre; when the book was published in France in 2011, Sinha lost her job. Juliana Delgado Lopera's groundbreaking *Fiebre Tropical* is written entirely in Spanglish. In its inventive and heady mixture of Spanish and English, Lopera captures a Colombian teen's arrival to Miami and uses language as a political tool to show how inextricably entwined the cultures of Latin America and the United States are. We're also delighted to publish the winner of this year's White Review Short Story Prize. Vanessa Onwuemezi's story 'At the Heart of Things' is a visceral journey into interiority and dreams. Formally daring and linguistically metamorphic, it is a worthy winner of a prize established to explore and expand the possibilities of the form.

Elsewhere, Khairani Barokka experiments with a hybrid of criticism and poetry by re-examining the figure in Paul Gauguin's famous portrait *Annah La Javanaise* through the intersecting lens of race and disability, before imagining new poetic futures for them. The psychoanalyst and writer Nuar Alsadir continues the theme of radical reinterpretation by applying Donald Winnicott's theory of the 'True Self' to mothering, writing and Anna Karenina. Anwen Crawford's 'All Circles Vanish' is an elegy to a lost friend and a deeply personal meditation on art-making and resistance – a resistance embedded within its unconventional form.

We are excited to present an interview with the American scholar Saidiya Hartman. Victoria Adukwei Bulley met her in London shortly before the publication of her newest and most ambitious book *Wayward Lives, Beautiful Experiments*. Hartman discusses how she started out wanting 'to be a witness': she has achieved this through her work in the archives, piecing together black histories through a technique she terms 'critical fabulation'. Tessa Hadley is one of the finest and most consistently satisfying British writers at work today; she talks to Sophie Collins about finding success late in life, and the difference between intellectual and emotional authority.

The artists Hannah Quinlan and Rosie Hastings contribute a series of photographs and drawings documenting LGBTQ+ social spaces around Britain, many of which are under threat of closure. As with all the writers and artists in this issue, critique is built into their perspective. Across these pieces, we sense a determination not only to replicate the world, but to render its complexity, violence and grief.

TESSA HADLEY INTERVIEW

There is something about Tessa Hadley's writing that exceeds intelligence. At once unadorned and meticulously put together, her prose seems to enact a refusal to acquiesce to beckoning dishonesties or white lies in the interest of a good sentence. (A refusal that, it turns out, makes for even better sentences.) When so much popular literature is drawn towards thought-terminating statements, phrases that sound good but mean little and, more importantly, fail to generate further thought, Hadley's fiction feels unusually frank and interrogative.

Her authorial commitment to verisimilitude frequently makes itself felt via narrative understatement, with delicate psychological shifts and idiosyncrasies taking precedence over revelation, confrontation. 'An Abduction', the opening story in Hadley's *Bad Dreams* (2017), follows Jane, a girl on the near edge of puberty, as she is picked up outside her house by three unfamiliar, significantly older teenage boys, and has her first sexual experience with one of them. 'What interests me in Jane's story,' Hadley has said, 'isn't the outward drama so much as her interior adventure... the frame of her world is wrenched.' Many years later, a therapist laments Jane's conventionality, her 'lack of imagination'; she will keep the events of that afternoon to herself, forever.

Hadley's most recent novel, *Late in the Day*, published earlier this year, maintains this interest in decades-long narratives and sudden drops in cabin pressure, in which her characters temporarily contradict their stated dispositions, act out. Christine, an artist, is married to Alex, a school teacher. Zachary, a curator, and husband of Christine's closest friend Lydia, suddenly dies, and these pairings threaten to invert – perhaps they already had. The milieu, as in much of Hadley's work, is markedly middle-class, something that is registered with candour and a certain irony. 'Their world was privileged, even in its grieving,' Hadley writes in the book, 'there wasn't any moral meaning to Zachary's death, it wasn't an injustice. And yet it undid them all.'

The changeability of her characters' lives is to some extent reinforced by the swing in Hadley's own course; she didn't publish her first book until she was forty-six. Before then, she looked after her home and children. Presently, she is the author of seven novels and three story collections, and is the winner of a Hawthornden Prize and a Windham–Campbell Literature Prize, among many other accolades.

On the day of our interview Hadley's husband Eric welcomed me into their flat near Hampstead Heath. He made each of us a cup of tea before disappearing. Hadley revealed herself to be a tactful, generous person; she put me immediately at ease. We spoke about John Updike, men and women, writing programmes, narrative, authority and the challenge of rendering visual art in writing. SOPHIE COLLINS

THE WHITE REVIEW   The way into your writing for me was through your reading of John Updike on the *New Yorker* fiction podcast. I usually hate to use 'translation' in this way, as a metaphor or simile, but when you were reading one of his later stories, 'New York Girl' – it was, for me, very much like reading a good translation, because after hearing it I wanted to read more of the author (Updike), but I also wanted to read the translator's work. Your work.
TESSA HADLEY   That's a lovely way of thinking about it. I'm so pleased, because I felt Updike was falling into disfavour and that people were – as I said in the podcast – carelessly writing him off and writing off a whole way of looking and seeing and feeling, which we shouldn't dispense with so readily. We have to be complicated about these things and not let some simplifying narrative override what is subtle and beautiful. Updike's story has got plenty of misogyny in it, plenty to unpick and critique. But bring all that difficulty on! Let's read it and let's live with it and know it, and then push back too.

TWR   I hate that thing of a protagonist's 'likeability' being an accepted measure of whether or not you're going to enjoy a book.
TH   Yes. It's quite in the air at the moment. Not just likeability but a kind of obedience to external criteria and a sense that we're allowed to like certain things and not allowed to like others. It's depressing sometimes. But every age has its own foolishness, and this is just going to be ours until it wears out and something else happens. There's a bit of puritanism in the air. Far better to read everything and anything and make what you can of it all, learn from it all.

TWR   When I read *Bad Dreams* (2017) I was so interested in the way in which you wrote about women. What struck me particularly was that there were women of different ages, at different stages of life and in different situations, but that you somehow made it clear to the reader that these were, in a fundamental kind of way, the same people, because they were each treated by you with such generosity, with an unusual degree of attention. Which meant also that each of their interiorities was entirely convincing.
TH   I think one of my favourites in that book is the very first story, 'An Abduction'. The narrator, Jane, is – to me – such an interesting woman, but she's outwardly dull. And that was my quest in writing it. To think deeply about somebody who looks from the outside like a boring person, with not much to give. If you'd met her at a party, say, you might have been looking to move on to talk to someone else. What I wanted to express, however, was how in her interior there might be a sort of locked cupboard of self with something saved in it. Something precious and significant which in her modesty she is actually in a better position to value than somebody much more sophisticated, somebody with a much more ready vocabulary of emotion and affect and intellection – the whole range of self, you know.

TWR   In that story, and in many of your other stories, and certainly in *Late in the Day*, there's a sense that the trajectories of the characters are entirely unpredictable; there are these air bubbles which open up and allow people to behave in quite strange ways, before suddenly closing again. At the end of that story Jane goes back to living a very conventional sort of life.
TH   Yes. She never tells anyone what's happened to her. She becomes a Tory voter just as she had said she would – and those clever boys were so amused by that. And when her own daughters grow up and start misbehaving as teenagers – I just sketched this in a few words – you know, she's quite strict and conventional. And it never occurs to her that in her own youth, once, she did those very things that she's now so disapproving of, frightened of. Her one night of crazy adventures is kept in her awareness in a separate, sealed compartment – which I do think some people do, with the most serious things that happen to them. They keep these things hidden and saved up. And then perhaps they will manifest later on. Perhaps the more conventional story is that these secrets will manifest as trouble later, something unresolved. But what if they're also treasure? Treasure *and* trouble.

TWR   And you can just keep them there.
TH   And you can just keep them. Of course that used to be a huge story for women. That they would have tiny little lives outwardly but inside them they'd have something so... *hot*. You know, like a radioactive thing. Alice Munro's brilliant on that. This crops up again and again in her stories, the idea that women who had incredibly limited lives – on a farm, not marrying, working the same household routine year by year by year,

hardly seeing anyone outside the family, living in the middle of nowhere – but they might have: one precious letter. And that letter would fill up a life with an intensity that somebody who goes off to Toronto, and takes their freedom, and has affairs with six different men, say, can only dream of. The Toronto-adventurer's accumulation of experiences may perhaps dissipate the intensity of feeling, of attachment. Nobody's advocating a return to tiny lives, certainly Munro isn't. You can't put the genie back in the bottle, no one can wish to go back inside that old simplicity. But in writing at least we can reckon with it, with its power.

TWR   Was it ever a conscious thing of wanting to expose, of wanting to talk about what is perhaps still specifically a female experience or way of processing? Or is that reductive? There's a lot of ambivalence in your female characters' minds... I feel they're quite mutable? A lot of things are constantly taking shape and shifting and forming – but probably that's not something you see as being unique to women?
TH   No. It can't be unique to women, can it? One knows enough lovely men who are mutable. Though maybe there's more mutating in women: for circumstantial reasons, probably, primarily. Women have been very adaptable. I was a housewife and a mother for twenty years before I was published. Writing, yes, but failing at it. Which wasn't a very happy experience. But formative. I wouldn't change it.

TWR   What do you mean by failing?
TH   Writing novels that were no good.

TWR   Did you send them out?
TH   I sent them out in a terribly blundering way. I knew nothing, really nothing about publishing. So I sent them to one publisher, not to an agent. There was one agent who I met once I moved to London. She didn't take me on but I met her. It was my most glamorous step at that point. But I'd send them to a single publisher, and then when they rejected them with pretty much a form letter, I would just take that to heart and think, well, they were right about it. So I wouldn't send it out to anybody else. But I'm so glad actually I didn't, because those novels were awful. I'm not sure I would wish all that disappointment and frustration on anybody, but for me it was the right thing, it somehow made possible the writing I was eventually capable

of. Eventually, in my late thirties, I did a Creative Writing course at Bath Spa University. I was very sceptical. I thought, none of the writers I love have ever been on a Creative Writing course – what is this *thing*? I don't believe in it. But on the other hand, I also thought, maybe I should at least just test this, this desire of mine to write. And if I'm really no good, then I have to stop because I'll be very miserable if I go on trying and failing – though I'm not much good at anything else, either. And the course was fantastic. Not because anyone can teach you to write. But because being on a course, talking with others, finding a community, having an audience – that's what makes the difference. It's also competitive: you have to feel, 'I have to do better than her.' 'That was quite good what he wrote today but not good enough, so write something that's better.' That competition lifts you. And you're also thinking, 'Those people are going to read this on Thursday and it's not protected enough. It's not smart enough, make it smarter. Make it cleverer.'

TWR   I was reading Bakhtin recently and he has the idea of the superaddressee, which is this sort of very critical but also benevolent voice that most people have on call, in their minds. I think when you actually go into a workshop it consolidates that voice. Makes it a real voice, for the first time perhaps.
TH   That's right. I had a superaddressee before I began the course but it was sort of... It was a bit nineteenth century. I was absorbed too much in the literary past, what I was trying for was too old-fashioned. Those old books are still the ones that matter most to me, or at least, as much as anything. But they can't be the whole of how you learn to write. You have also to write for now, for the present.

TWR   Your books are so emotionally intelligent. Do you think that there might be an issue with publishing fiction very young, in that you might not have yet acquired enough experience to properly pierce such things?
TH   It depends. I think it was true for me. I was so sort of receptive, but without authority, for so long. I had authority intellectually, but not emotionally. So I was very assured in my critical judgements, but I wasn't very assured in my emotional or imaginative worlds, and I was far too much in awe of some imagined critique. So,

yes, for a long time I don't think I had enough to say because I actually didn't know what I thought. I thought a thousand things, and I didn't know which one I *really* thought. If I read anybody and liked their work, then I was completely persuaded by them. I was very impressionable. I still am! – but I also have a mastery of what impresses me now. I don't have a particularly good memory, and I think that's because I take in a thousand little bits of information and at first they don't cohere very well. For instance I'm not very good with people's faces. And I think it's because I see too much at once, too many different aspects, which don't cohere at once into a pattern. I think this is why it took me a long time to settle down in writing. But I'm talking about me, and you asked a much more general question. I think there are writers who are ready when they're young, they have that authority, to seize the pattern at once through all the impressions. It's a good job some writers are ready when they're young. In the nineteenth century so many of them were dead by the time they were thirty-six or forty-six. They didn't have our leisure to soak up life slowly. The Brontës. Or the young D. H. Lawrence, he was a marvel. It's a good job he didn't wait to begin until his forties.

TWR   Does a novel feel like a testing ground for certain perceptions, of certain personalities?
TH   It does... It does. Actually this new one of mine, *Late in the Day*, I'm beginning to realise now just how personal it was, in testing certain ideas and possibilities. Not that it is in any way the story of my life. But I was testing out things about women and art, Christine's sense that her work is at the centre of her life – and then her doubt about that, when Zachary dies and she seems to have lost the power to make anything, to believe in it. And then there's Lydia's different bet, on sex against everything else in life – what might a beautiful woman do with that risky bet as she got older? So yes, that does feel as if I was pushing lots of ideas which are important to me, in quite a testing way. But mostly when you're dreaming up the subject for your next novel, planning it, you're developing its form aesthetically rather than through its ideas. You're thinking, 'That will be rich; that will be a good story to tell.' 'That story's full of *heat*,' you think. It is as if certain stories and scenes as you begin to imagine them give off warmth. They've always been there in potential, somewhere in your imagination, but when you focus on them you

suddenly think, 'That's just got such a lot in it, it's so rich with possibilities.' So the one I'm just starting, a new one, is set in 1967, when I was only a child – it's not so close to me as *Late in the Day*. My heroine is quite a heedless woman, absolutely not an intellectual or an artist. All of my characters in *Late in the Day* are quite clever and bookish. In this new book, mostly unwritten as yet, the men – in time-honoured fashion – are informed and intellectual, but my heroine is a forty-year-old, happy, easy, good-looking suburban housewife. And she's going to do this crazy thing and go off with a young student: and through him she'll encounter the whole modern thing, revolution and politics and freedom. I had a picture of her in one scene literally having her mind forced open: just by talk that makes her see everything, her whole world, her whole life, differently. The young man is quite careless and offhand, opening up all these ideas to her: it's just the easy shorthand of his set, their conversational small change. But there she will sit, thinking about the world in a new light – it's a conversion story, almost like a religious conversion – the Vietnam war, capitalism, injustice. He wants her to come to bed then and she won't, she just has to sit there, she can't sleep or lie down. At some point, of course, her daily life resumes. But this revelation will have changed her completely. Both her own life-adventure and then the whole cast of her family and friends dealing with what she does, her rash act – that seemed a very rich story to me.

TWR   Does the overflow of the current project seed the next?
TH   I think it must. But it may be, 'When this project's finished I'm going to do the absolute opposite.' So *The Past* was three weeks in the country with one set of people and then *Late in the Day* covers decades. It's always a reaction to the one before.

TWR   In *Late in the Day* Christine talks about Paula Rego. Are you drawn to any written work that operates on a more surrealist or symbolist plane than your own?
TH   Somewhere deep down in my childhood formation, I've always inclined towards realism. Even when I was a tiny child, I preferred the children's books that were about a family living in a house in an ordinary street and going to school, rather than the fairy tales. I did read the fairy tales, but warily, with some fear, and some – tedium, perhaps? My

husband loves folk tales and fairy tales – we have quite a collection of them. But in the end I always wanted to step across the threshold of fiction, not into what's mythic but into the illusion of daily lived life, in real historical time. It's just temperamental, just taste; intellectually I fully appreciate the magnificence and the necessity of what's mythic in art. I really love Paula Rego's work and find her so interesting – and of course she's not a naturalistic painter in any ordinary sense. And yet however fantastical some of her paintings are, deploying her private and weird symbolism, they always also seem to me to take place in real interiors, actual rooms, during particular periods of history. Her characters are individuated people. I think I'm slightly bored by fictions that don't work to create the illusion of life-likeness.

This question of art's illusion of life is central for me. At some point in the history of fiction, instead of the old kind of story that said, 'The miller had three sons, and the third son wasn't left anything when the old man died and he went off to make his fortune in the world. He made seven friends and one of them could…' Instead of that – or a serious religious parable about a prodigal son, say – we began to tell this kind of story. 'It was seven in the evening and snow began to fall. A carriage rolled up outside,' and so on. Once you've done that thing – which I suppose began in Europe, in the eighteenth century – once you've brought into being that possibility of creating in words on the page an illusion of daily reality, it's such a wonder, has such power over our imaginations, that you can't ever quite put it away again. We can't easily unlearn, as readers, our appetite for it. It's an aesthetic development comparable perhaps to the invention of perspective in the visual arts. Once perspective is a possibility, even if an artist chooses not to use it, he or she has deliberately *not* used it. The power of the illusion of felt, actual lived life in a baggy novelistic form is a sort of marvel to me, joyous. And it's something I've been addicted to since I was quite a small child.

TWR   What do you think about the assertion that the omniscient narrator ought to have been left at the end of the nineteenth century?
TH   I like to use an omniscient voice sometimes. I feel it's a resource of the fictional fabric that is probably a bit underused at the moment. Writers who play experimental games with form use it more than the realists, perhaps. Writers of

psychological realism tend to go for an interior voice, a close third person, absorbed in a character's thoughts, not seeing them from outside. For a while we associated omniscience, probably rightly, with a kind of nineteenth-century overconfidence about the way the world was. But there are ways of using it which don't entail that over-confidence. Elizabeth Bowen, who's one of my heroines, is a useful model here. She uses an omniscient voice often, with its implication that 'You have crossed the threshold into this fiction, and I am describing to you this landscape as if it's real, and yet there's no doubt about it, I am a writer and I'm writing these words down, and I'm not trying to pretend I'm not here, telling you these things. I know everything about my characters that I choose to know, that I choose to put in here, including what they can't know about themselves.' And at the same time as seeing her characters from outside she can also drop down deep inside their very intimate thoughts and intimations. It's a wonderfully flexible narrative positioning.

Omniscience is too good a resource to leave behind. And there are lovely ironised ways we can use it now to make our truth-claims in fiction. More tentative truth-claims, perhaps, than in the nineteenth century. But we are the god inside a novel. We can know everything about our world and characters that we want to know, and can choose to tell it to our readers or not tell it. So it's a kind of pretence, in a way, to write as if 'all these characters are actually real and I'm just letting them speak, I'm not really here'. Of course I don't disapprove of that pretence in the least – fiction is all pretence! – and lots of sublimely good things have been written out of that submersion in character, avoiding omniscience. And I'm sympathetic to the hesitation which says: 'We are no longer omniscient because we don't have those kinds of truth certainties any more.' But it's also possible to sidestep any overweening truth-claims by putting the writer's omniscience at the front of the narrative, overtly. An omniscient voice can mean that we aren't pretending that the writer isn't making all this up.

TWR   When you were writing *Late in the Day* did you think much – because there's so much engagement with visual art – around the idea of ekphrasis? Something you seem to be really conscious of, which I appreciate, is the limitations of text when it comes to describing art, and I feel like your way around that, in the book, is to just talk, in quite a pure way, about the characters' responses to the artwork, eliding an omniscient or ostensibly objective view.

TH   I had to work out how to do that, how much was I going to say about Christine's work. I knew I had to say something. But I didn't want to circumscribe it or go on about it too much. I thought there was a way of hinting at what her work was like, and her career, but not overdoing it, summing it up in little bits of throwaway. I had to convey how huge it was in her life: but at the same time I needed to leave a gap around her pictures, rather than describing them too literally.

Often you're not making a theoretical decision over something like that – over my description of the Tiepolo ceiling, say. You're just reading the scene through. And I will have written too much about the painting, and it's just reading clunkily, like 'Oh, suddenly I'm in a catalogue description.' The language is wrong, the feel of it is wrong, it's letting the truth of the story down. So it's the aesthetic of the scene, in the end, rather than a kind of pre-existing decision about proportions, that makes you cut. And it's all to do with the flow of the scene. You write and read, and then write and then read, and then write and read. Just trying to read it as if you hadn't written it. 'Is that right now? Is that it? Do I need a tiny bit more? No.'

It's what an artist is doing, I suppose, when they stand back from the canvas and wipe that bit of the white off and then they stand back again, and then they put in a little bit of green, and then they stand back again. Which is why nobody can teach you how to write, but what they can do is stand creatively behind your shoulder, saying 'I love this, but here it's gone off. And I need more of this. Make this bit better, just here.' This is what a teacher's response to a writing student feels like, I think. All the input is so specific to the particular story, to the writing on the page.

TWR   That bit about the Tiepolo ceiling which Christine and Zachary are so stirred by is in sharp contrast with a later scene where Christine goes to see an exhibition at the gallery after Zachary has died. And I think he's compared this artist's work to hers?

TH   He has. He said, 'You'll love it', and now he's dead, so that message seems very important to her. She's gone charged up with feeling for her dead friend, expecting to find something that speaks to her in the exhibition. She thinks it's going to be some sort of fulfilment, like a last word. And then she's bored by the paintings, she doesn't like them, they don't interest her. I knew I was going to end with that scene – it's almost the end, not quite – before I even started writing the novel. I thought it was funny as well as poignant. I love ironies like that. That you would expect some great culminating encounter with the man who's dead and you really loved him, and now he's speaking to you through these paintings. And you go all primed up for that, and instead you think, *'But I don't like them.'*

TWR   'He doesn't know me.'

TH   'He doesn't know me.' I loved writing about Christine and her art. We don't ever know, of course, in *Late in the Day*, whether she's really any good herself, as a painter. That remains an open question. We can't see her paintings. We know she's serious about them. We know that Alex has his doubts, and we're probably quite cross with him for having them. But who knows, in the end, maybe he's right? I mean that's just open, isn't it, in the fiction as it might be in life. What's really any good? Zachary loves Christine's art but she thinks that actually he loves too many people's work – he's a gallery owner, he has to. I'm interested in Zachary's generosity in judgement, and also in its opposite in Alex, who is asserting his mastery somehow with his 'no', his doubt. 'Oh no, you can't do it like that.' It's such an interesting power dynamic, that critical negativity. Its unkindness and power-move can't be separated from its truth, sometimes. And Christine is full of judgements too, often negative ones.

TWR   Although Alex is a slightly unqualified master.

TH   He is indeed.

TWR   He terrifies me actually!

TH   Does he terrify you?

TWR   Yes. He was like a composite of men that I know or have met.

TH   I'm pleased to hear that, in one way... That verifies the possibility of him. He's certainly like a composite of certain men that I have met. But I had wondered whether they don't make men like that any more. Only every time I've said that—

TWR   They definitely do.

TH　—young women have said, 'They definitely do!' But perhaps they're on borrowed time now. And perhaps we will miss them, if one day they're gone, with their gift of mastery, their ferocity. Their rightness, on occasion. At the end of the novel, you know, I think I gave Alex quite a happy ending. I think he's learning a different wisdom, as he's growing older. He's got this time left to him after his friend's death, and there's a sort of tenderness towards Lydia, at the end, that is new. He's making his bargain with time and ageing and after all he doesn't pursue those two other women who cross his path, where something might have happened.

TWR　The one really generous moment towards Lydia from Alex is when the narrative enters into his having had this disdain for her self-effacement. Or, it's not exactly self-effacement, it's seen more as a sort of languidness. And now he sees it as an almost religious undertaking.

TH　Yes, he comes to see that a certain fatalism or passivity in a certain kind of woman – Lydia has been content just to *be*, not to *do*: to be beautiful and admired and loved – which he used to think was trivial and stupid, has its magnificent aspect. Almost religious, yes. Dedicated: filled up with time passing rather than trying to control it, commandeer it. I spent a lot of time writing that passage, because that idea interested me so much. It was much longer originally than the little bit that's left, because it took a lot of working out: I'm so pleased that you noticed it. Perhaps it connects in some way to what we were saying about the short story 'An Abduction'. Lydia is nothing like the woman in that story, but I am interested in people who don't *act* or try to make a mark in the world, but nonetheless accumulate power and *life*. Lydia is very unlike Jane. But they share a kind of fatalism. They don't examine themselves but submit to what happens to them almost passively. Lydia knows the risk she takes, betting her life on love, like a nineteenth-century romantic. She knows what she is. I like her for it. I admire her. Alex learns to admire her too.

S. C.,
May 2019

FIEBRE TROPICAL
JULIANA DELGADO LOPERA

FICTION

Buenos días, mi reina. Immigrant criolla here reporting desde Los Mayamis from our ant-infested townhouse. The air conditioner broke. Below it was the TV, the flowery couch, La Tata half-drunk directing me in this holy radionovela brought to you by Female Sadness Incorporated. That morning as we unpacked the last of our bags, we'd found Tata's old radio. So the two of us practised our latest melodrama in the living room while on the TV Don Francisco saluted *el pueblo de Miami ¡damas y caballeros!* and Tata – at this age! – to Mami's exasperation and my delight, went girl crazy over his manly voice.

Y como quien no quiere la cosa, Mami angrily turned off the stove, where La Tata had left the bacalao frying unattended, then Lysol sprayed the countertops, smashing the dark trail of ants hustling some pancito for their colony behind the fridge. Girlfriend was pissed. She hadn't come to the U S of A to kill ants and smell like puto pescado, and how lovely would it have been if the housekeeper could have joined us on the plane? Then Mami could leave her to the household duties and concentrate on the execution of this Migration Project. Pero, ¿aló? Is she the only person awake en esta berraca casa?

On the TV, another commercial for Inglés Sin Barreras and Lucía, La Tata, and I chuckled at the white people teaching brown people how to say, *Hello My Name Is.* Hello, I am going to the store. Hello, what is this swamp please come rescue us. It was April and hot. Not that the heat dissipated in June or July or August or September or even November, for that matter. The heat, I would come to learn the hard way, is a constant in Miami. El calorcito didn't get the impermanence memo, didn't understand how change works. The heat is a stubborn bitch breathing its humid mouth on your every pore, reminding you this hell is inescapable, and in another language.

We'd been here for a month, newly arrived, still saladitas, and I already wanted to go back home to Colombia, return to my panela land, its mountains and that constant anxiety that comes just from living in Bogotá. That anxiety that I nonetheless understood better than this new, terrifying one. But Mami explained to me over and over again with a smirk that, look around you, Francisca, *this* is your home now.

Our to-do list that doomed Saturday of the ants and the bacalao included helping Mami with the preparations for the celebration of the death, or the baptism or the rebirth or the something, of her miscarried dead baby, Sebastián. It has been argued – by the only people who care to argue: La Tata and her hermanas – that my dead brother's baptism was the most exciting event in the Martínez Juan family that year. This mainly because La Tata drank half a bottle of rum a day, couldn't tell Monday from Friday, so obviously a fake baby's baptism at a pastor's pool was more important to her than, say, the fact that by the end of that month my younger sister, Lucía, was regularly waking in the middle of the night to pray over me. Or the fact that I would eventually remember this time, the first months after our arrival, as Mami's most sane, grounded moment.

Pero we're getting ahead of ourselves, cachaco. Primero la primaria.

We'd been prepping for the baptism celebration even before departing from our apartment on the third floor down in Bogotá. Inside the six Samsonite bags that Mami, Lucía, and Yours Truly were allowed to bring into this new! Exciting! think-of-it-as-moving-up-the-social-ladder! life were black-and-gold tablecloths, hand-crafted invitations, and other various baptism paraphernalia. There wasn't enough space for the box of letters from my friends or our photo albums, but we nonetheless packed two jars of holy water (instead of my collection of CDs – The Cure, The Velvet Underground, The Ramones, Salserín) blessed three days before by our neighborhood priest, water that was confiscated for hours by customs (*You don't think we got water in the States?*) then quickly flushed down the toilet by Tía Milagros, who now soaking in Jesús's Evangelical Christian blessing believed, like the rest of the Miami matriarchy, that Catholic priests were a bunch of degenerados, buenos para nada. Catholicism is a fake *and* boring religion. Christianity is the true exciting path to a blessed life in the name of Jesucristo nuestro señor, ¿okey?

Now Mami hustled her bare butt around the dining room, head tilted hugging the telephone, wearing only shorts and a push-up bra, fanning herself with a thick envelope from the stack of unopened bills. Anxiously phoning the Pastores, the incompetent flower people (*Colombianos tenían que ser*), the two lloronas in black – Tía Milagros's idea – who would professionally mourn Sebastián while charging Mami fifteen dollars an hour.

Miami wanted a dead baby's baptism, motherfucker, and Mami was gonna *give it*.

Homegirl didn't see anything wrong with chipping away – I would find out later – at our life savings by buying tears and feeding the congregation.

Pero – óyeme – you couldn't fight her. Esa platica ya se había perdido. Esta costeña estaba montada en el bus already. Mami never got a break. Never stopped to smell the flowers. Cómo se te ocurre. From the moment we arrived, Myriam del Socorro Juan was on her crazed trip to *get shit done*. We were handed to-do lists; we were yelled at, directed; we were told what to do every single step of the way.

We were obedient. What else could we do? Where else could we go?

The outskirts of Miami is dead land. It is lago sucio after dirty lake with billboards and highways advertising diet pills and breast implants. With almost nonexistent public transportation, no sidewalks, but a glorious Walmart and a Publix Sabor where a herd of colombianos, who came all the way from their land, buy frozen arepas and microwavable Goya plantains. Lucía wasn't complaining. La Tata barely had strength to fight Mami. The surrounding swamp collaborated with Mami to make every single day excruciating.

Pero, mi reina, siéntate pa'trás – we're only getting started.

For the last month, we'd been pushed around from this church service to that church dinner to that church barbecue. Meeting this hermano, that hermana, and that very important youth leader. We'd listened to our tías spill all the church tea over and over again during lunch and dinner. Even during onces they wouldn't shut up. Everyone arguing over who was a true Christian and who was just calentando silla. I quickly figured out that there's a lot to being an aleluya daughter of Jesucristo and that attending church on Sundays was just the tiniest tip of the faith iceberg.

My dead brother's baptism was part of the iceberg. Dead babies need to be baptized, mourned, and named so their souls don't linger, so they, too, join the fiesta celestial. This was part of La Pastora's explanation, and Mami just nodded with her hand on her chest saying, Ay sí, el dolor es tan grande.

Now La Tata and I eyed each other as we watched Mami's frenzy torbellino around the living room. Mami going on and on about all of the items on the to-do list that we still hadn't done or didn't do the way she wanted. Tata and I wanted to hold Mami's hand, tell her, Ya ya, Mami. Come on now, Myriam, carajo, deja el berrinche. We wanted to slap her a little because we still believed underneath that new layer of holiness there was the pious Catholic neurotic we'd known so well. Tata and I had some serious eye-to-eye magical power going on. I knew she needed a rum refill when her left eye went *Give me a break* and she knew I was this close to slapping Mami when my eyes went *Buddha shut*. After signing the divorce papers, Mami had rolled around for three days with the same crazed energy she had now, painting our entire apartment in Bogotá a tacky red then crying because her house resembled a traqueto's wife. And when that wasn't sufficient to kill her mojo, this cartagenera costeñita de Dios bleached Lucía's and my hair with hydrogen peroxide because na-ah! No hombre is going to ruin Mami's life, not even your father. In those moments she was too gone inside herself, too deep in her darkness. Glossy-eyed, pale, making endless to-do lists, and yet her hair was always blow-dried, impeccable.

Y ahora there was no man but a dead baby who needed to be baptized inmediatamente. Y ahora Lucía helping Mami with the final touches on the cake: the black-and-gold icing underneath the Jesús in the plastic cradle retrieved from the pesebre box. Tata frying the bacalao in the kitchen, yelling at no one (but of course at Mami) that, pero claro, Myriam doesn't have any birthing hips no wonder she lost a baby. If she heard her, Mami se hizo la loca. If she heard her, she did her usual deep breathing, deep sighing, did not bother with Tata.

Then Lucía sat next to me on the couch. Her tiny legs next to mine. The TV still on, but we paid no attention. We sat staring at the ceiling fan, drooling, captivated by its speed; the hum of the blades both terrifying and quieting, drowning out the sound of Mami and La Tata, giving us a break. The possibility of it breaking and cutting us all to shreds. Lucía and I did this often. We never had a ceiling fan in our house in Bogotá, we never needed one. But here we sat side by side in silence staring at it, mesmerized by its movement. I concentrated on the sound, a little motor promising wind. A short relief from the heat. Lucía smiled at me and I felt a sudden rush, wanting to hold her tight, kiss her curls, place my head on her shoulder. Instead I just turned around, closed my eyes, pretended I was somewhere else.

*

Between phone calls Mami gave us The Eye: the ultimate authoritative wide-open flickering of lashes with an almost imperceptible tilt of the head that had us on our feet and running. She did the same thing whenever the nuns sent home a disciplinary letter back in Bogotá, searching for my guilt, and I tried to resist, daring myself to withstand The Eye for as long as I could but always failing. This time, we were too exhausted to resist. We were exhausted from moving our shit around. Exhausted from meeting this youth leader, that former junkie church woman (*¡La drogadicta encontró al Señor!*); every señora de Dios fixing our hair, squeezing our cheeks, commenting that we were either too skinny, too fat, too pale, or – my very favorite – too Colombian (*Cómo se les nota que acaban de llegar, tan colombianas*).

The 'too Colombian' comment offended Mami. Being too Colombian meant it was evident that her hair wasn't blow-dried every other day; our rough edges were showing, o sea, criollas, o sea Mami didn't even understand ni pío of English and that threw her in the bottomest of the bottoms of the hierarchy. All she could say was, Yes yes cómo no. But I was 15, coño, qué carajo too Colombian. I didn't care if I was too Colombian. To me, everyone was too Colombian and that in itself was part of the problem. All I wanted were my girlfriends back home, cigarettes, and a good black eyeliner. None of which Miami was giving me. Instead it gifted you with an infierno that crawled deep into your bones and burned its own fogata there. A surreal heat that veiled everything, like looking through gas, all of it a mirage that never dissipated. A stove burning from within. I didn't want to admit it to myself or anyone but I was pure Soledad Realness, pure loneliness eating at my core. Dándome duro. Did living with La Tata help? Did living close to Milagros and my other tías and primos and the freaking Pastores and that señora from the congregation who always brought us arepas and called me La Viuda (*Toda negro siempre, Francisquita, como La Viuda*) on Sundays? Did this aid the transition in any way?

Falso.

It made it worse. Their enthusiasm was unbearable.

Because this wasn't a Choose Your Own Migration multiple-choice adventure where a, b, and c are laid out at the end of each page and you can simple choose (b) Stay in Bogotá, you idiot. Cachaco, please. This was militant Mamá Colombiana popping Zoloft, begging your daddy to sign papers, then finger waving at you to pack your bags while she sold your remaining books, CDs, the porcelain dolls nobody wanted; as she donated your Catholic school uniform (that you hated, but still), locked herself for hours inside the bathroom with the phone and a calculator and then emerged puffy-eyed informing Lucía and your sorry ass that ni por el chiras, you were not leaving in six months but next week because Milagros got Mami a job (that never materialized), and then *boom boom boom* some Cuban guy speaking condescending English stamped your passport, shot Mami a smirk-smirk for those boobs – he literally said *boobs* – and when she asked you to translate you simple said, Ay Mami, pero you didn't know people speak English in the U S of A?

Óyeme, la cosa no termina ahí.

Porque what did we really know about migration, mi reina?

I knew nada before forever jumping across the Caribbean charco. You kidding? This homegirl lived in the same apartment on 135th Street, next to the same tiny green patch that passed for a park, next to the chapel where I got fingered by two boyfriends; the same Cafam supermarket, the same corner store where Doña Marta sold me cigarettes religiously under the same excruciating Bogotá smoggy clouds. Complaining about traffic every single day for the entirety of my fifteen years. We were so anchored in Bogotá, so used to our homogeneity, that the girl in school from Barranquilla – the only girl in school from outside the city – was an exotic commodity. The girls at school made fun of her ñera ways, the way her mouth ate all the vowels as if only for our amusement. And although Mami is originally from Cartagena, she moved to La Capital when she was 16, losing her costeña accent. We only traveled to the Cartagena coast on vacation, once a year, which in itself was the Event of el Year (planned for months) and caused enough commotion to last until our next visit: ¡Las maletas! ¡El pancito for your tía from that special panadería! ¡El sunblock! Etc. New haircut, blowdried hair, and new (awful, hated forever) sunflower dress with matching gold communion studs worn to impress the epicenter of the matriarchy.

Every trip felt so painful because Mami didn't (and still doesn't) like change. She likes to stay put and, if possible, very still so nothing moves. Anything new sends her on a rollercoaster of anxiety that she, por supuesto, denies and hides very well. She's obsessed with routines and systems, lists and crossing things out with a red pen when they get done. The day we left Bogotá the stress casi se la come, a rash of tiny red bumps grew on her back and she didn't stop scratching until the señorita flight attendant said, Welcome to Miami.

*

A few days before the baptism, Mami arrived with a huge yellow dress for me. Yellow is such an ugly color. Plus I hated dresses. Mami knew I hated yellow – and red and orange and all warm colors. You know what was yellow? My Catholic school uniform. Freaking pollito yellow with orange stripes and a green sweater embroidered with the initials of the school and a tiny brown cross. The nuns made sure there wasn't the slightest possibility of provocation or desire that could awaken the evils of boy temptation, which only existed outside of school, while we respectable teenagers – an endangered species – were protected by the tackiest, most unfashionable piece of clothing ever invented. As if someone's barf had become the color palette of choice. Men didn't piss on us to mark territory, we had the nuns to thank for that. And now here it was, that dreaded color popping up in my life again in the form of a baptismal dress inside a Ross bag coming to me via Mami's exhausted joy.

Le dije, Mami ni muerta am I wearing that dress– She stopped me halfway and said, You haven't even looked at it closely. It is so bello, ¿verdad, Lucía? Look how bello y en descuento. You haven't tried it on, nena. Try it on, ven pa' acá.

Ay Mami. In my heart I knew the dissonance my body felt every time I wore a dress, a kind of stickiness. But Mami's face is Mami's face, and I nonetheless removed my black shirt, my shorts, and right there in the living room surrounded by all the porcelain bailarinas and their broken pinkies, I became once more a sad yellowing sunshine. I looked like a lost kid at a parade. Yellow dress, dirty white Converse.

Mami first said, Francisca, why aren't you wearing a bra? Horrible se ve eso. Followed by, Who taught you not to wear a bra? And then, Ay pero mírala, how pretty. Your grandma can fix the sides but it fits you perfectly.

Tata and Mami discussed the alterations on the dresses. Mami bought a red one for Lucía and a black mermaid one for herself, a gorgeous piece, but with tiny holes around the neck pointing at its 50 per cent discount. It is true that Tata and Mami shared an unimaginable love for Jesucristo, but it is *also* true that their deepest connection was the sale racks at Ross, the coupons at Walmart, and the impossible variety of pendejadas para el hogar at the dollar store. And, reinita, don't even get me started on Sedano's. The discounted world of chain stores a sudden miraculous revelation. The world may be coming to an end but at least there was nada nadita nada you couldn't get for under five dollars *if* you looked hard enough, *if* you knew where to go, on what dates, and what coupons to bring. Mami and Tata memorized the entire sales calendar of all their favorite stores, and once a week out they went in Milagros's borrowed van to do the family's shopping, which brought us stale bread, rice with tiny squirmy friends, and pompous dresses from Ross with holes around the armpits.

Tata will fix those – was Mami's answer as I stared into my dotted armpits. She dismissed my concerns, treating the needle-and-thread process as her own personal designer moment; as if the holes were not there because part of the dress had literally been eaten by moths but because it was an unfinished masterpiece waiting to be completed by Mami's unique fashion vision.

Parezco un cake, I said.

She chuckled. You look bella, like you used to when Tata sewed your dresses, remember?

I didn't say anything because it was *pointless* to fight her over this, plus as much as Mami angered me back then there was also that face of hers suddenly brightened by the baptism. Still, I stood in the living room – as Tata took measurements, placed pins in the dress – staring at the horizonte in front of me with the martyr look I'd learned from my tías; my eyes looking to the side slightly, as if about to cry but holding it all inside; it was Virgen María's suffering meets Daniela Romo's anger meets a Zoloft commercial. A pose that I will use over and over again throughout my life. A pose passed down through the generations of female sadness stacked inside my bones, all the way back to Tata's mother's mother. A pose that says: I'm here suffering pero no no no I do not want your help; I want you to stand there and watch me suffer – witness what you have done – and let me suffer silently, with my discount glam.

Outside, the sky in all its fury released buckets of water that swayed with the palm trees. El cielo gris, oscuro. Talk about goth. Right at noon the sky transformed itself from orange light to chunky black clouds that gave zero fucks about your beach plans or the three hours you spent ironing that hair, splaying all its sadness right in front of you. Washing you with its darkness. Right before the rain, the humidity intensified, the soil-smell mixed with garbage-smell almost unbearable. Sweat a constant, all the way to my butthole. Dampened skin, fishlike. Water came from all places: the ocean, the sky, the puddles, our armpits, our hands, our asses. Our eyes. Lluvia tropical is nature's violence. And here it was a lluvia tropical on acid, a fiebre tropical. Tropical fever for days. Nature soltándose las trenzas, drowning the ground so that by the evening, when the rain subsided, the land turned into a puzzle of tiny rivers, small ponds where worms and frogs alike built homes and where Mami's feet and pantyhose sadly met their demise several times. More than once, she arrived at the door mojadita de arriba abajo, not wanting any help but just yelling at me, Por favor por favor, to look at her feet and remove any animalitos.

¡Tengo bichos por todas partes! she'd say, disgusted. And I would try to help even though she said she didn't need any, but of course I'd remove the worms and beetles stuck to her pantyhose; I'd bring a towel, dry her hair, comb and braid it. All the while she kept saying she didn't need anything.

What I need right now is for you to look at this sorpresa I found, said Mami toda happy, all the attention on the larger-than-life Ross bag.

¡Tará!

Out of the bag she pulled a naked baby doll with blue eyes and a swirl of plastic black hair. A beat-up Cabbage Patch Kid like the ones I begged for when I was younger, but this baby had seen some truly rough days: the cheeks shadowed with dirt, the left eye missing part of its blue, the skin a worn light brown.

Pero this was only the beginning, cachaco.

Then came the tiny set of little boy's clothes: pants, shirt, even a black tie.

Why ask her? Why ask her when you already knew the answer? Nevertheless there was an urgency inside me to have this crazy Jesucristo rollercoaster ride echoed back at me so that I knew I wasn't losing my shit. So that I didn't doubt my own reality. *This is happening, right? Mami* is *laying out a doll's outfit on the couch, she* is *tying her hair back with a scrunchie, she* is *fanning herself with the receipts, she* is *ignoring me when I ask the following question: Mami, what is all of this?*

Either homegirl didn't hear me or was too enveloped by the muñeco now trying his new baptismal couture. She placed the doll on her lap and with great care, dressed the piece of plastic with the tiny pants, the tiny shirt, and the tiny black tie. The gender of the doll was questionable – equal amounts of blue and pink – and my insides chuckled thinking Mami was dressing a girl doll in boy drag. So much for that beloved son! I questioned his gender out loud, but she didn't care. She could have been dressing a giraffe – it was her lost baby and she loved him.

¡Encontré a Sebastián! she announced with such enthusiasm.

Who would have thought my dead baby brother would come back to us via discarded toys in the sale section at Ross. Who would have thought he would come back at all.

Doesn't he look like he belongs to the family? She chuckled. Then sensing the silence continued, A little rough, yo sé, but nothing a few damp pañitos can't fix.

She had a point. The only big difference was most people in the family had a heartbeat.

It was then my turn to nurse the fake baby, carry him in my arms. You know, I used to love my dolls when I was a peladita. In my own way. I chopped their hair, drew trees and clouds on their bodies. I searched incessantly for their genitals. My Barbies would sit around drinking cafecito waiting for the one Ken Man to show up and whisk them away, but Ken Man would take so long the girls would inevitably get bored, get hungry, and eat each other's hair, sometimes their limbs; sometimes they drew tattoos on their bodies; other times the Barbies fucked their golden retrievers. My Barbies' children consisted of Legos, pencils, and a little squirmy hamster by the name of Maurito. No human children allowed for my girls.

Take the baby! Mami handed it to me. Take it, carajo, que no muerde.

I grabbed the doll by its head, a little disgusted by the thing. But Mami wasn't having it.

¿Es mucho pedir? she said. Too much to ask that you not handle him like he's trash?

I wanted to say, *But he is trash.*

Instead, I angrily hugged him tight while Mami continued explaining that of course he's not a real baby, Francisca, ¿sabes? He is a symbolic bebé, ¿sí? Like Jesús is not really in our hearts? It is a *metaphor.*

She kept talking about the flesh-and-bone baby. Said something about his soul, his eyes, something about the dress for the baptism, but I wasn't listening. I heard the Venecos blasting music outside, Lucía blasting Salvation upstairs, and the rumbling of the air conditioner trying as hard as it could to not let us die in the heat. Then I remembered Mami's white scar. The squiggly milky river dividing her lower belly that I traced with my finger when I was a kid. The one exposed right now cause she's heated, almost en cuera; the one she pointed to every time we needed a reminder of all she'd done for us. They chopped me up, she'd say, this one is *you*.

Standing below the ceiling fan, I locked eyes with Tata, who winked at me and mouthed, Tenle paciencia a tu mami, then patted my hand so I would refill her rum.

Before I could say anything Mami turned to me. Are you listening?

I wasn't.

Obvio que sí, Mami. I'm right here, I told her, holding Tata's hand.

Women in my family possessed a sixth sense, not necessarily from being mothers, but from the close policing of our sadness: Your tristeza wasn't yours, it was part of the larger collective female sadness jar to which we all contributed. Your tías could sense your tristeza even before you sensed your tristeza. As if the arrival of sadness shed a specific smell only detectable by the leonas; the older the leona the more masterful, the quicker she detected your soul stinking up the place. They pointed at your sadness to make theirs more secretive and therefore grander. Epic. Yes yes, you're sad, Francisca, but how about your Tía Milagros working twelve hours under the sun? How about your Mami losing a baby? Losing your father? How about that? I have countless teenage memories in which my sad emo adolescent body didn't even get a chance to relish in its tears, to soak in the obliqueness of a dark life, because there was always a tía yelling from the couch as I stepped into the living room: Ay pero here she comes with that face. Ay pero si acá no ha pasado nada.

Rapidito. Faster than they could sense their hairs curling up before the rain.

Inevitably now, Mami turned to me and said, Ay pero what's with the face? Cualquiera diría that you're having a bad time. But you're not nena, so brighten up. Deja la pendejada.

HANNAH QUINLAN AND ROSIE HASTINGS

Between 2015 and 2016, artist duo Hannah Quinlan and Rosie Hastings travelled the UK documenting the interiors of LGBTQ+ social spaces – sex venues, community centres, bars and clubs. The archive they produced, UK Gay Bar Directory (UKGBD), documents cultures in peril. Over the past decade 58 per cent of LGBTQ+ venues in London have shut. The trend is reflected across the country: the result of a cocktail of rising rents, the advent of sex apps, the effects of austerity on spending habits, and a generation who find the old-school, gender-conforming gay scene, which has long dominated the LGBTQ+ sphere, exclusionary and incompatible with contemporary queer politics and tastes.

Caught between mourning for communities under siege, and reckoning with emotional questions of access and belonging, UKGBD speaks to the difficulty and necessity of finding solidarity in fractious times. Increasing numbers of people have begun to identify as queer, attracted to the moniker's promise of inclusivity and self-determination. Yet this upsurge is taking place alongside the erosion of space and tolerance. UK politicians are once again openly questioning the morality of teaching LGBTQ+ lessons in schools, threatening to plunge us back into the dark ages of the 1980s and 90s, when Section 28 banned state schools and libraries from suggesting that homosexuality was 'acceptable as a pretended family relationship'. The same rhetoric historically used to smear gay men as predatory is also routinely mobilised to denigrate trans people in the name of feminism.

For *The White Review*, Quinlan and Hastings present photographs taken as part of UKGBD, as well as a selection of drawings the artists began making in 2017. Geared towards grandeur, the drawings are hymns to queer sociality, in which muscular, gender-ambiguous characters hang out in bars and clubs, or attend parties and protest marches. Bodies are given heroic proportions, and compositions borrow from Renaissance painting. Stylistically the works echo the 'gay aesthetic' popularised by the mid-century homoerotic comics of Tom of Finland – reveries of men in uniform with impossibly meaty bodies. Only in Quinlan and Hastings's drawings, the explicit, carefree sexual dimension has dissipated, and every smile is charged with anxiety. The 'is that a truncheon in your pocket or...' fantasy has been replaced by something more complex: a world in which dreams of queer utopia are laced with the potential for violence and loss.

PLATES

VIII

II

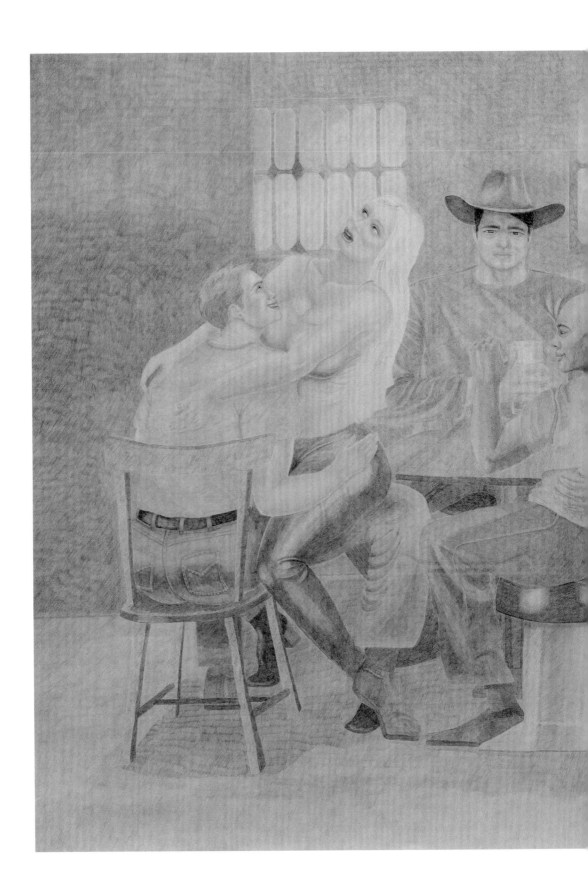

GBOYEGA ODUBANJO

DALSTON LANE

we huddle by the upstairs window   face the noise
  a street song kettled and screeching its own broken
yes

      we could watch it on the tv but do not trust
the definition of its bodies still learning how to move to
this noise that scratches on them   skipping
so we look

         my father is first to turn
he steps outside and squats on the roof of his car
throwing shiny objects onto the floor distracting
                    those who might approach him

my sister follows with a bucket
and a sponge   she washes the road of all its glass
and its blood   tells us that it is her glass and her blood
  refuses help

         my brother is stapling himself
to the street signs   my sister is washing his blood
which is her blood also   my brother has stretched himself
so wide around the noise and is checking everybody's papers
as they enter

         my mother stands on the corner of every road
in her arms is a book of names that she has given
and must give to the noise
  i stand behind her   holding her hand   waiting my turn
the noise is blurred big and still i am not knowing how to move

DRAKE EQUATION

i'm running out of data on the train everyone is feeling particularly lonely
    it isn't enough
everyone & me ear plugged & stirring is listening to something
considering charts & cadence of feet bounce it is likely we are listening to
Drake

Drake says sometimes i feel good sometimes i don't

he knows that until he bursts from carbs or cliché we will love him always
Drake has been on our minds now for some fourhundredtwenty weeks at least
everyone & Drake is wearing t-shirts with Drake lyrics printed on them
we are signing love letters and suicide notes with Drakeisms it isn't enough
wake up mumbling something Drake drool on our pillow wonder where else
still
    we can find traces of him
    we're only now just learning

Drake says more life more everything
    always more feeding every hour
    on the hour
    all the amenities
    the biggest residential pool
    on the planet
    everybody in it
    my critics & my friends
    fat happy house
    my children &
    everybody loving me
    the pictures
    portrait of the artist
    eating portrait
    of the artist in
    the biggest residential
    pool on the planet
    fat & happy
Drake's ear is to the zeitgeist listening for something out there
shooting his shot into space waiting
    it isn't enough
to hold everybody
& their faces sing it
there are so many people

outside that haven't heard it
yet i don't know if
they can wait   how long
Drake says   i do not know
        what permanence is
i'm only now just learning
i'm upset   doing the best that i can
to be heard
i need more content

ECLIPSE

              so moon turns now
       turns dark & new
              to self   embraces shade
       is pulled
              it pulls itself sick
       sick itself of turning
              of vinyling
       its croon   it turns
              as coon
       turns kinte   trades limb
              for tongue
       sits bust pretty
              plinth happy
       turns still & slow & true

MORPHINE
NUAR ALSADIR

ESSAY

One day, while I was preparing dinner at the kitchen counter, my daughter, then six, who had been playing at the kids' table behind me, approached, glanced at the vegetables on the cutting board and said, 'That's going to be horrible. A horrible dinner.' She turned, walked back to the little table, sat on a small wooden rocking chair decorated with yellow ducklings and added matter-of-factly, 'Mommy, I hate you.'

Without responding, I continued preparing the horrible meal. Ten minutes later, after rocking back and forth in her chair, singing, kneading clay, she called out tenderly, 'Mommy, I love you.'

'First you hate me,' I said, 'then you love me—'

'Mommy,' she cut in, rapturously, 'I everything you!'

One of Donald Winnicott's most important contributions to psychoanalysis was the idea of a 'holding environment', an atmosphere that communicates to another person – a child, a patient in analysis, a lover – that whatever they express will be accepted: the good, the bad and the ugly. Having the space and opportunity to be fully oneself gives a person the chance to become a self, as opposed to an assemblage of feelings and behaviours they have been conditioned to adopt in exchange for affirmation or love.

A former patient of Winnicott's, Margaret Little, described a moment in her analysis in which, feeling utter despair, she 'attacked and smashed a large vase filled with white lilac'. The next day, when she showed up for her session, she found that 'an exact replica had replaced the vase and the lilac', letting her know that nothing had changed. A holding environment creates the security necessary for a person to express their impulses and intuition, rather than to act on the strategic desire to manage how they are received.

There is comfort in letting go, being able to be yourself without the risk of rejection or losing love. The desire to feel held and contained – emotionally swaddled – is a primal instinct. When feeling Margaret-Little-level despair, my daughter used to crawl under the kitchen table and sob, 'I want to go back into my mommy's belly!' The comfort in being held inspired Temple Grandin to invent a hug machine, a concrete holding environment used to soothe and contain autistic children. Winnicott recognised not only how crucial the sensation of being held is in the development of a child, but how necessary it becomes for the feeling to be recreated in an analytic setting, particularly for someone who did not experience it often enough during childhood to recognise who they were before having to adjust that self to social demands.

Is it mere coincidence, then, that Winnicott's father, the father of the father of the holding environment, was a merchant specialising in women's corsets? A corset holds with inverse objective – to tuck away rather than spill over – and is used to hide flesh, an excess of body – being *too much* – with the aim of avoiding critical judgement. Fathers in Winnicott's theories – those trafficking in the corsets of laws, codes and regulations – are largely absent.

Mothers (or primary caregivers), on the other hand, at best, encourage their small children to express themselves freely by remaining receptive to all communications, however vicious or wild. A baby who cries or bites and is then punished for being bad will learn to restrain themselves in order to access the rewards that accompany good – which is to say, desired – behaviour.

Giving the mother what she wants in exchange for affirmation and care is the only way a baby can control her environment. In fact, '[t]here is no baby,' according to Winnicott, 'only a relationship.' Because all babies need a caregiver to survive, they quickly learn to adapt to maternal demands – a tactic that gets carried over into adulthood, even though it is rarely literal survival that is at stake.

Someone who perceives early on that moving things around on the outside (making their mother feel good) is a way of moving them around on the inside (feeling loved themself) is likely, later in life, to use people, objects and substances as vehicles to modulate their feelings and thoughts. This basic principle is encapsulated in the precept, 'It's not what you know but who you know' – an inevitable dynamic in infancy when one's agency is at the mercy of the mother. But what is for some a phase to grow out of can, for others, become calcified into a belief system, particularly if receiving care was connected to gratifying the demands of others in childhood.

Of course, every parent has to set boundaries that will feel, when curtailing freedom, like demands. One of the most difficult parts about being a mother is snuffing out my children's impulses, teaching them to disconnect from their interiors in order to display proper behaviour (*inside voice, don't stare, pretend you like it even if you don't*). It is my ultimate maternal duty to watch over their survival – literal and social – but also to guard over their connection to their spontaneous instinctive selves, so they remain emotionally alive as well.

◀

Anna Karenina is a book of orphans. Anna, herself, is an orphan. Tolstoy makes no mention of her parents, only two aunts: one who brought Anna up and another who freeloads off her while she is living with her lover, Vronsky. We know nothing of Anna's childhood or early adulthood, or what her life was like with the aunt who raised her, beyond the fact that she pressured the tedious but dutiful Karenin – Anna's husband (also an orphan) whom she left for Vronsky – into marrying her niece by making him believe his honour was at stake. He complied with what was asked of him, in exchange for a respected position in society.

Their forced match not only locked Anna into a loveless marriage, but into a life that placed appearances over desires and needs, the external above the internal. The impression Anna's sister-in-law, Dolly, had 'of visiting the Karenins' – Anna and her husband – was that 'there was something false in the whole cast of their family life'. The 'False Self', according to Winnicott, is a persona put forward that conforms to the codes and expectations of others at the expense of what he calls the 'True Self', the deepest core of our being, the part of us that feels 'alive' and 'real'.

The True Self in an infant is communicated through spontaneous, nonsensical gestures, which the mother will either accept or correct. If spontaneous expressions are permitted without judgement or alteration, the infant will receive the signal that it is safe to express herself, but if they are corrected, the infant will be trained to bypass impulses and reach for learned expressions instead – the first step in the development of a False Self.

We all have false selves – it is necessary to have a protective skin in order to go out into the social world. The False Self, in fact, shelters the True Self. But a False Self so fortified by layers of compliant behaviour that contact is lost with the raw impulses and expressions that characterise the True Self often results in a person feeling as though they don't really know who they are beyond what is signalled about their interior through

the ideas, interests, friends, and achievements they have accumulated from
the outside world.

When I first read *Anna Karenina* in high school, I was captivated by Anna,
who is all of light. Tolstoy introduces her to us through Vronsky's eyes as
'so brimming over with something that... showed itself now in the flash of
her eyes, and now in her smile'. I aspired to be Anna, wondrously lit yet
'[d]eliberately... shroud[ing] the light' even as 'it shone against her will'. As
she comes into contact with Vronsky's force field, 'the joyous light flashed
into her eyes', and he, too, felt the pull.

'Isn't it amazing when you see someone who has the light?' Oskar
Eustis, Artistic Director of New York's Public Theater, recalled a friend
asking him after seeing actor and clown instructor Christopher Bayes
perform for the first time. He relayed the comment during a toast at
Bayes's recent book launch, and the clowns in the room – all having been
transformed in some way by Bayes's light – nodded emphatically. As with
Proust's underground, once a certain way of being has been cognised,
you recognise it everywhere.

The light was the wax lining the paper cup of my childhood. I remem-
ber lying on the floor of an attic room in a high school friend's house
during a party, staring at the whir of a ceiling fan as the boy I'd been
involved with told me over and over (he was on shrooms), 'We're burning
people... burning people.' I didn't need to be high to know what he meant.
That burning had drawn me to him in the first place, though I'd never
put it to language.

Transmissions that cannot be explained logically pass between people
all the time, though only some give them attention. When Vronsky first
glimpses Anna, he feels 'the need to glance at her again – not because
she [is] very beautiful' but because of 'an abundance of something', a
'radiance', that 'overflow[s] her being'. That something – radiance, light
– has less to do with looks than a living energy emitted by 'anyone', as
clown guru Philippe Gaulier's definition of beauty has it, 'in the grips
of freedom or pleasure'.

Because this beauty flows outside the circuit of social currency, it is
unlikely to be apprehended by those unattuned to its frequency. Tolstoy
seemed ambivalent about whether value could be given to passion that
was not above ground, connected to social mores or religion. 'Eruptions
of sexual desire cause confusion,' he wrote in a notebook, 'or rather
an absence of ideas: the link with the world is lost. Chance, darkness,
powerlessness.' Can we trust desire if it cannot be transposed onto an idea,
linked to the logical world? And can a character – a woman moreover –
who chooses to leave her (dreary) husband and beloved child to pursue
passion be permitted pleasure and light?

Even as Tolstoy allows Anna to be all there, he punishes her for it by
making her unable to control her light when it's not refracted through a
socially sanctioned structure: what had 'brimmed over... against her will'
begins to blaze, and, though '[h]er face was brilliant and glowing', this
glow 'was not one of brightness; it suggested the fearful glow of a confla-
gration in the midst of a dark night'. Chance, darkness, powerlessness.
In Tolstoy's hands, the light led to Anna's suicide – a death that served as
a warning, what might become of me as well, if I didn't shroud my light.

Anna Karenina becomes a morphine addict. Throughout the second half of Tolstoy's novel, she uses morphine to drug her impulses and spontaneous expressions because she worries revealing parts of herself that her lover, Vronsky, doesn't like might cost her his love.

The novel's famous suicide scene is preceded by her having taken a double dose of morphine. In a delirious state, 'everything that had seemed possible to her before became difficult to grasp'. With ambivalence and last-minute regret, she throws herself before a train and dies.

Even as she manages her happiness, which is dependent on Vronsky's being happy with her, by numbing her emotions, Anna recognises that those very emotions are connected to what is most valuable in her: '[s]he found it painful for these feelings to be stirred up, but she nevertheless knew that this was the best part of her soul, and that this part of her soul was rapidly being smothered in the life she was leading'. Strong emotions – although sometimes painful or confusing – make us feel alive. If we suppress them to avert unpleasant sensations – or to avoid inducing them in others ('People', my mother used to say, 'want to be around happy people') – we become detached from our interiors and a sense of falsity or deadness ensues. 'Can I call this living?' Anna asks herself. 'I am not living... I'm restraining myself... it's all deception, it's all just morphine under another name.'

The motivation behind such restraint – corseting any sense of aliveness – is to quiet the anxiety that accompanies it, as Winnicott explained in a letter to an American correspondent:

> if you are "all there" then sooner or later this anxiety beyond what you can tolerate comes over you, and you cannot hold it long enough to look at it and see what is the content of the anxiety. If you could do this you would find that it contains – at root – the deepest source of your own psychic energy, so that when you have to blot it out (or it happens to you that it gets blotted out) you lose the taproot, so to speak.

When we allow ourselves to be 'all there' – for all of ourselves to be present, even the difficult, fleshy, unwieldy aspects we fear exposing to the criticism of others – we become anxious, and in our desperation to quell our anxiety, we reach for a shroud, morphine – whatever quick fix might protect us from a painful emotion even as it blots out the best part of our soul, the taproot, our deepest source of psychic energy.

Anna could 'only suppress terrible thoughts about what would happen if [Vronsky] stopped loving her with activities during the day and morphine at night'. Morphine proper or by another name allows us, like Anna, to be there without the risks associated with being all there, but also without the benefits of feeling on, fully present, alive. Whether with opioids, alcohol, work, exercise, socialising, or other forms of distraction, we all, at some point or another, find a substance or activity to fill our minds so there is little room left for troubling thoughts or emotions to set in.

Though uncomfortable, anxiety is a signal from within that can be useful if you can 'hold it long enough to look at it and see' that it contains 'the deepest source of your own psychic energy'. Rethinking our ideas about disquieting emotions allows us to tap into alternative energy sources. For example, the unsettling changes that stress creates in the brain and body, explains psychologist Kelly McGonigal, make us more 'alert, raw, vulnerable [...] open to the world around [us]'. Tolerating these feelings long enough to harness that 'surge of energy that is encouraging [us] to engage' will help us muster the strength to 'rise to a moment that matters'.

◪

'Only the True Self can be creative,' wrote Winnicott, 'feel real'. The hallmark of a false self, by contrast, is a lack of 'creative originality'. The capacity to be creative develops out of a sense of being safely held in a reliable context that makes it safe to *everything* one another, to be all there, flesh-out, able to access the taproot, that deepest source of psychic energy, in ourselves and others.

Anna is a thinker, reader and writer of great intelligence. She has 'remarkable knowledge' of architecture, machinery – topics she discusses confidently with the men at her and Vronsky's table. She speaks 'in a natural, clever way' and 'read[s] a great deal – both novels and the serious books [...] foreign papers and journals'. Anna's brother describes her to his friend Levin, the character based on Tolstoy, as having 'inner resources'. She even wrote a children's book, he relays, that a publisher described as 'remarkable'. Then, looking at Levin's reaction, he adds, 'I can see you are smiling ironically, but you're wrong.'

Levin isn't the only character that doubts the intellectual capacity of Anna and women in general. One of Anna's major fights with Vronsky occurs when he makes fun of girls' high schools and women's education more widely. Anna is offended because she sees it as an allusion to her own reading and intellectual pursuits, even as she is the one who does research, the intellectual legwork, for his projects. Anna downplays her knowledge, artistic capabilities – likening, for example, her writing to basket-weaving – in order to minimise anything that may threaten or elicit ironic smiles from those around her. Anna's behaviour is choreographed to manage the impression others have of her – a False-Self concern that dampens the creative process, which hinges on an artist's connection to her internal world.

◧

Bobbie Louise Hawkins, a poet and prose writer of the Beat generation, was married to the poet Robert Creeley for eighteen years. 'When Bob and I were first together, he had three things he would say,' Hawkins recalled:

> One of them was "I'll never live in a house with a woman who writes." One of them was "Everybody's wife wants to be a writer." And one of them was "If you had been going to be a writer, you would have been one by now." That pretty much put the cap on it. I was too married, too old and too late, but he was wrong.

Complying with these precepts would prioritise external demands over internal drives. At a recent tribute to Hawkins at Saint Mark's Church in New York, Eileen Myles relayed an anecdote Hawkins liked to

> She would tell this story and then she would smile and that was really
> the last line, where it was just like, there was an element of triumph...
> Bob and Bobbie had gone out and Lucia babysat for them... and I think
> Lucia was in her aspiring writer mode and writing, and she had given
> Bob some work. So he was driving her home after she babysat and
> on the way home he pulled over under this tree and she thought,
> "Oh, he's going to talk to me about my work." And they sat there for
> a moment in the moonlight looking at this tree, and he said, "Lucia,
> see that cottonwood tree?" And she was like, "Yeah, Bob." And he
> said, "Be like that tree for your man."

Hawkins and Creeley eventually divorced, and Hawkins pursued
her artistic ambitions while teaching for many years at Naropa. At Saint
Mark's Church, Reed Bye recalled sitting in on a class Hawkins taught,
in which she advocated for 'the virtue of surprising turns that short circuit
discursiveness'. A surprising turn takes you off the moving walkway,
and, like an infant's spontaneous gesture, brings you back to impulse
and intuition:

> She ended the class with her paraphrase from a poem by Lew Welch,
> "Small Sentence to Drive Yourself Sane". And the poem:
>
>> The next time you are doing something absolutely ordinary,
>> or even better
>>
>> the next time you are doing something absolutely *necessary*,
>> such as pissing, or making love, or shaving, or washing the dishes
>> or the baby or yourself or the room, say to yourself:
>>
>> "So it's all come to this!"

"Like, whatever you're doing," Bobbie said, "just stop in the middle
of it, look around and say, 'So it's all come to this.'"

Anna tried to be that cottonwood tree for her man, but the more she
suppressed her emotions, the more they built up and pressed for release.
Because Anna's husband, Karenin, wouldn't grant her a divorce, she and
Vronsky lived together in a relationship society wouldn't sanction, and
were not accepted as a couple into the social world. Vronsky, however,
was granted admittance on his own, while Anna, completely cast out,
could only see people when they visited her. Vronsky genuinely loved
Anna, was willing to give up being firmly installed in society to be with
her, but wasn't willing to lose, in Tolstoy's words, his 'male independence'.
He was trained from an early age to prioritise external demands over his
emotions, and therefore remained ambivalent about completely giving
up the rewards society offers to those who follow its codes.
    When we first meet Vronsky, we learn that 'in his soul, he did not
respect his mother, and, without being conscious of it, did not love
her, although in keeping with his upbringing, he could not imagine his
attitude to his mother being anything other than extremely obedient

and deferential'. When his mother tries to undermine his relationship with Anna, his obedience to her is pitted against his love. Anna, perceiving this, panics, tries to turn Vronsky against his mother by speaking disparagingly of her, in order to keep him from going to see her. Vronsky asks that she 'not speak disrespectfully about [his] mother', aligns himself with the demands of his upbringing, but, unable to corset herself, Anna ramps up her attack.

When Anna is *all there*, Vronsky, rather than being able to offer a holding environment in which he tolerates her full range of emotions, says, 'No, this is becoming unbearable', gets up, tells her his 'patience [...] has limits', and walks out to see his mother. Anna takes a double dose of morphine.

In her delirious state, 'everything that had seemed possible to her before became difficult to grasp'. With ambivalence and last-minute regret, she throws herself onto the train tracks. Like Margaret Little, Anna had smashed a vase, but unlike Winnicott, Vronsky wasn't able to withstand her despair, replace the vase – communicate to her that she's more important than the vase, the prohibition against breaking it – and remain present.

The 'destructive aliveness of the individual', writes Winnicott, 'has vital positive function'. Winnicott explained the 'positive value of destructiveness' in his radical, groundbreaking paper 'The Use of an Object'. It is essential, he says, for the infant to destroy the mother in order to move from a primitive narcissistic relationship (in which the mother is recognised solely as a means of getting needs met) to a more mature relationship (in which she's understood as a separate person, possessing her own mind). It is when the infant is ruthless towards the mother and sees that the mother is hurt – rather than angry or frustrated, which is how the infant feels – that she is able to recognise that the mother has her own emotions, existing outside of the infant's omnipotent control. Because the mother has her own feelings, she is separate; and because she is separate, she is real. It is only then, in the mother's realness – not as a projection, but as a separate subject – that she can become available for what Winnicott terms *use*.

If the mother retaliates, she is feeling the infant's feelings – which, in other contexts, is a useful mode of communication, but when the destructive feelings (despair, rage) elicit the same destructiveness in turn, the infant has got inside the mother's head and is controlling her from within. That degree of power is terrifying to a child because, if the mother is an extension of the infant and not a separate person, she is not only incapable of being used, but a mere projection, and thus unreal, which is to say, not really there at all. The mother needs to demonstrate that she is separate and real, all there, which she does by tolerating the infant's being all there as well.

For a mature relationship to exist, two individuals must encounter one another in their separateness, which is established once they become available to each other for use by surviving a destructive attack ('"Hello object!" "I destroyed you." "I love you." "You have value to me because of your survival of my destruction of you"'). It is when one person is able to recognise the other's independent existence that the other becomes real and seen – and, in feeling seen, becomes real to themselves as well. It is only when two individuals come together as separate that they can love and be loved.

'We never fight,' psychoanalyst Danielle Knafo records a new patient telling her, describing his two-year relationship. 'She's not the kind of girl who could ever give me reason to fight with her.' He went on to explain how this relationship was different to his two marriages or that of his parents, in which his father had 'nothing left of his manhood' – or, in Vronsky's terms, 'male independence'.

People often mistake a lack of conflict for a working relationship – the way a baby who doesn't fuss is deemed 'good'. Not infrequently, when I'm working as a psychoanalyst, a patient will say that their partner has asked them to talk to me about going on antidepressants. When we explore the request, we find a hope that the antidepressant will make the couple's problems go away by subduing the feelings behind the tension, much as Anna hopes morphine will do for her relationship with Vronsky.

The perfect girlfriend described by Knafo's patient – the woman who met his needs without compromising him in any way – was a high-end sex doll. These dolls, which have become increasingly popular across the globe, are life-sized human figures covered with flesh-like silicone rubber and equipped with both vaginal and anal orifices fabricated to 'feel real' without the mess of interiority.

Feeling real, however, is not that simple. In order to feel real, a person has to have had the opportunity to express themselves spontaneously without worrying about losing love. An infant, according to Winnicott, feels real upon seeing recognition register in his mother's face, which is different from looking into a mirror and seeing his own reflection. The infant must feel real before being able to recognise the reality of another person, which is grasped when they are seen to exist outside of the infant's omnipotent control. If the infant perceives that the mother has the capacity to feel an attack (she has her own emotions) and can survive that attack without retaliating (it's okay to express oneself), the mother will have been, as Winnicott puts it, *found*. Through finding the other, one finds the self.

V

My younger daughter's first word was *mama*. Mama was a name, but also a word attached to me that meant *I want it, get it, give it to me, I hate it, I'm about to attack*. A couple of months later, rather than calling me *mama*, she began to use the name *Mimi*. It seemed like an odd regression, until one day I heard in her enunciation our combined selves: *Me* (her self) and *Me* (my self, which was also hers): *Me-Me*.

Oedipal representations – when a child is four or five – are vastly different. At four, my other daughter called me over to look at a drawing she'd made of our family. There were four figures: a little girl, a littler girl, a father and a cat. 'Where am I?' I asked.

'Here,' she answered, handing me her pencil. 'You can draw yourself.'

When working as a psychoanalyst with patients whose issues are pre-oedipal – which is to say originate in a developmental phase that is primarily prelinguistic and merged – it is necessary to tune in to communications that are transmitted outside of words. An experience that occurs before words are available will register in non-rational, imagistic terms within the body, as opposed to linguistic, rational ones – making it more difficult later, after language has been acquired, to recollect and communicate the memory in words than through images and sensations.

When an adult relationship involves merging, it replicates that early relationship between mother and infant, in which the other person does not fully exist, but functions as a vehicle towards getting needs met. The stakes are likely to feel connected to survival, as they did in infancy, prompting desperation and compliance to kick in, along with the restraint of any part of the self that seems too risky to express. Genuine spontaneous expression will always involve a degree of risk.

I use a wooden match as a bookmark.

'Who can say,' Winnicott quotes Pliny asking, 'whether in essence fire is constructive or destructive?'

Winnicott, who was based in London, presented 'The Use of an Object' for the first time on 12 November 1968 at the famous New York Psychoanalytic Institute, where the predominant approach to psychoanalysis did not then involve much consideration of the period in development during which non-verbal communication predominates. The paper took many surprising turns – in a way Bobbie Louise Hawkins would appreciate – veering sharply away from the thinking of the discussants and using terms that were common to them in defamiliarised ways. Winnicott broke ground and they retaliated.

After he finished giving his paper, the discussants subjected it to ruthless attacks. Winnicott responded by telling the group that 'his overall concept had been torn to pieces and he would be happy to give it up'. The vase had been shattered and no one was there to replace it or pick up the pieces. He went back to his hotel room that night and had a heart attack.

Bringing one's deeply creative projects to light is a way of exposing the True Self, which most people – out of a desire to protect what is most precious – keep hidden. Though Winnicott's health improved, he never fully recovered and died two years later.

Still, as I imagine it, Winnicott would not have felt regret. ('Oh God!' he wrote in 'Prayer'. 'May I be alive when I die!').

I overhear my daughters in the next room:

Daughter 1: I can't believe you flushed my barrettes down the toilet! They were my best ones.
Daughter 2: I know! They were so cute!
Daughter 1: How could you?
Daughter 2: [cheerfully] I was so angry.

'It is perhaps the greatest compliment we may receive,' wrote Winnicott, 'if we are both found and used.'

'[L]ook at your aggressiveness,' Winnicott wrote in a letter, 'it provides one of the roots of living energy.' If you numb aggression, like suppressing anxiety, you may avoid conflict with those around you, but you'll also lose access to the taproot, the ability to feel creative, alive, connected to others, real. By harnessing your living energy – aggressiveness, anxiety, primitive destructive impulses – you can, as Kelly McGonigal suggests, 'use some of this energy, use some of this biochemistry, to make choices or take actions that are consistent with what matters most'.

What if Anna had not been, like Tolstoy, an orphan, and had experienced a holding environment in her early life? What if she had been in analysis with Winnicott rather than a character in Tolstoy's narrative? What if, alternately, she had been placed in the hands of an author who granted her permission to feel and express her emotions fully?

On the first page of Elena Ferrante's *The Days of Abandonment*, we learn that the main character Olga's husband has left her. Every subsequent page offers the reader an unmediated sense of the emotional and physical struggle that ensues. Olga tries to make herself appear beautiful to rekindle her husband's desire, and conceal the fact that 'the life had been drained out of [her] like blood and saliva and mucus from a patient during an operation'. But falsity doesn't sit well with her. Unlike Anna, who dresses up, wears make-up and takes morphine to align herself with Vronsky's desire, Olga can't swing it. She becomes depressed and fluids – from tears to menses to bile – begin to seep out from her interior:

> [I]mmediately I felt depressed. My eyelids were heavy, my back ached. I wanted to cry. I looked at my underpants and they were stained with blood. I pronounced an ugly obscenity in my dialect, and with such an angry snap in my voice that I was afraid the children had heard me.

Storytelling, writes Ferrante, 'gives us the power to bring order to the chaos of the real under our own sign'. But when the sign controlling the narrative comes so frequently from outside of us, we 'internalis[e] the male method of confronting and resolving problems [... and] end up demonstrating that we are acquiescent, obedient and equal to male expectations'. Feminine narratives have the potential to express a different kind of order. By removing the corset of laws, codes and regulations, each individual body and narrative is free to spill over, take its own direction and shape.

Feminine narratives, it is important to note, are not limited to women, just as male methods are not utilised solely by men. Internalised masculine methods, in fact, often cube men with greater intensity than they do women. 'In order to live a fully human life,' wrote Adrienne Rich, 'we require not only control of our bodies (although control is a prerequisite); we must touch the unity and resonance of our physicality, our bond with the natural order, the corporeal grounds of our intelligence.' The natural order, like our corporeal intelligence, is not gendered or socially coded.

When Olga's husband judges her outburst of emotion through standards of behaviour – one should not get angry in front of children – and asks her, as Vronsky asked Anna, to change the way she was speaking, she responds uninhibitedly:

> I don't give a shit about prissiness. You wounded me, you are destroying me, and I'm supposed to speak like a good, well-brought-up wife?

Fuck you! What words am I supposed to use for what you've done to me, what you're doing to me? What words should I use for what you're doing with that woman? Do you lick her cunt? Do you stick it in her ass? Do you do all the things you never did with me? Tell me! Because I see you! With these eyes I see everything you do together, I see it a hundred thousand times, I see it at night and day, eyes open and eyes closed! However, in order not to disturb the gentleman, not to disturb his children, I'm supposed to use clean language. I'm supposed to be refined, I'm supposed to be elegant! Get out of here! Get out, you shit!

Olga's rage, like Anna's, was followed by an exit.

e

Near the elevator of my office building is a sign: YOU ARE HER EXIT. The sign makes me think of Anna Karenina's predicament. I wonder what it would have taken for Vronsky to have been HERE rather than HER EXIT – to have been all there, which is to say fully present, and, in the present, not *there* but *here*. What does it take – not only for Vronsky, but for anyone – to be *all here*?

The simple answer is an *e*.

In mathematics, *e* is known as Euler's number, an irrational figure, about 2.71828. It exists in mathematics, physics, nature – and I'd like also to imagine a metaphorical equivalent in interpersonal relationships. This imagined application of *e* would offer a way of addressing the irrational component that is necessary in experiencing a connection as alive and real.

What Winnicott terms the 'True Self', Audre Lorde would call 'the erotic' – our 'physical, emotional, and psychic expressions of what is deepest and strongest and richest within each of us'. Yet we are raised, she says, to fear this energy, marked by 'non-rational knowledge' – 'the *yes* within ourselves, our deepest cravings' – because it threatens the social system, which is not based on primal impulses, or the body, but on logic and power. A sense of non-rational bodily aliveness marks one's having accessed the wellspring of living energy marking the True Self.

Love is irrational – if you can explain it, it's likely an illusion. And it is precisely this irrational component that creates radical possibility. Even as it was progressive of Anna to leave her husband and live with her lover, she realigned herself with dominant structures in using morphine to numb the best parts of her soul as a way to avoid the loss of Vronsky's love.

The corset brings rewards, the positive gaze of others, but also stifles contact with the taproot, restraining one's ability to feel creative and alive. Lorde champions the power of erotic non-rational knowledge because it taps into an energy that all radicalism must harness. Every move that feeds the False Self – places external demands over internal desires – may protect the True Self, but will invariably strengthen the system that pushed it into hiding in the first place. 'The master's tools,' as Lorde puts it, 'will never dismantle the master's house'. It is the surprising turn, spontaneous gesture, that short-circuits discursiveness, brings forth the light that allows us to look around, see and be seen. It all comes to this.

LET'S KNOCK OUT THE POOR

SHUMONA SINHA
tr. SUBHASHREE BEEMAN

THE WHITE DESIRE

Weary and overwhelmed, I let myself fall on the clammy floor of the cell where I'm locked up. My thoughts are still with the people who invaded the seas like discarded jellyfish on foreign shores. We received them in semi-opaque, semi-transparent offices. I was one of those in charge of translating their tales from one language to another, from the language of the asylum seeker to that of the host. Bitter and cruel tear-flavoured tales of winter, dirty rain and muddy roads, tales of unending monsoon as if the sky burst open.

A few months ago, I had slammed the door on my boyfriend and my work. It was a year of break-ups, penury, a lack in everything. I lived in a state of irritation and confusion. The city seemed to have closed in on itself. The doors were heavy again. Large, green, latticed wooden doors with iron handles that time had smoothened and darkened – they didn't move under my hands any more. At times, I pushed them with my entire body as if I was holding up a sinking boat. But the city doors remained closed to me.

And then I was called for this interpretation job. There, the men looked similar. Their tales resembled other tales, no difference except for details like date and name and accent and scar. It was as if a single and unique story was being recounted by hundreds of men, and the myth had become the truth. One single account of multiple crimes: thefts, assassinations, aggressions, political and religious persecutions. They were woeful *tusi-talas*, *tusi-talas* despite their woes. To my ears, their stories seemed diced, chopped, spat out. The men memorised them by heart and vomited them in front of the computer screen. Human rights do not include the right to survive poverty. Besides, they had no right to mention the word poverty. A grander reason was needed to justify political asylum. Neither destitution nor the vengeful Nature that devastated their country could ever justify their exile, their wild hope for survival. No law would allow them entry into this European country if they did not claim political reason, or even religious, if they did not demonstrate severe sequelae to persecutions. Therefore, they had to hide, forget, unlearn the truth and invent a new one. The tales of migrating people. With broken wings, dirty, stinking feathers. With sad, rag-like dreams.

Dream is an early recollection. Dream is this desire that makes us cross thousands of kilometres, borders, seas and oceans; it projects a splash of the colours and hues of another life onto the grey screen of our brain. And these men invade the sea like discarded jellyfish and throw themselves on foreign shores.

FROM THE OTHER SIDE OF THINGS

The offices where the wretched asylum seekers came to plead with tired feet, alone or carrying children in their arms, were located in neutral and empty areas of the city, in the peripheral zones. Beyond the red line. Here, the wind picked up. The wind picked up, quietened and picked up again. The dust flew and spun around. The field was set ablaze. Here was the noise of the RER, its corroded grating, iron against iron, sprawling crisscross of railway lines up to the horizon, toward starker zones, shards of sunlight on railway lines, factories erected against blue sky. Old hands of the city, artists and rebels, librarians, bookshop-owners, teachers and activists, liked these hidden places. They felt proud discovering another face of their city, one that is more secretive, more underground, less flamboyant, but *where life is what one makes of it, where life abounds, and where the heart beats once again*, they said. But the country's leaders were not alive to the charm of these neighbourhoods under construction, or already in abandon. They felt that these areas were good for building gloomy offices to receive a mob that was not of this country, that could never belong to this country. The kind of mob that could not mingle in the chic neighbourhoods of the city.

Exiting the suburban railway station, you had to turn left. Cross the damaged tar road, avoid puddles and the grey-and-green barriers indicating ongoing construction work. The road sloped down, bypassing the steps and lawns. A bearded chap had chosen a part of the steps as home. His Alsatian dogs rested, tongues hanging out. The man scribbled on a piece of paper. On closer inspection, you could notice that he was relentlessly working on a sudoku in an old newspaper. Green letters. Dirty and wet pages. The road continued under the bridge. Many lanes converged into a single road. One palm with fingers spread. The RER passed overhead. The water dripped from the bridge's concrete underbelly, naked and surly. Then the void overwhelmed. On the left, unending buildings, large and ambitious, the tension hidden behind the glass mirrors, the towers erected like a wall. Across, the wind picked up. The highway swallowed the steady stream of cars and spat them out on the other side of the ringroad. The wind played, became more malicious as it hit the walls of buildings. For a moment, it looked like it was dead. It came back more fiercely than ever, from some part of the empty and staggering veranda between the building's two towers. The road swerved left again. Now, for the first time, you could see chaotic queues of desperate people. They formed groups based on their countries of origin. They were darker than their afternoon shadows. Together, they resembled an unexpected large cloud that could pour down on the city at any moment. The wind finally died with them.

Within two steps was the door to privileges. To those who decide. To those who help to decide – language gymnasts, legal interpreters. To those with neither a cloud nor a shadow on their face. They, too, have long wandered before arriving here, their lucky country. Their lives intermingle like paths cluttered, paths that descend to the dark knots of history. But the language gymnasts have realised their goal. They have crossed the barbed wires and no man's lands, troubled waters, stormy skies, administrative counters; they have proved their merit, their legitimacy, they have fought and they have come out victorious. Their burden, their baggage was not only in the aircraft hold, but also on their shoulders. Invisible, heavy, dirty. Or in their stomachs, like an overdue foetus, whose delivery would be painful, bloody, failed. They hide them, mask them without knowing it and try to learn the new social codes. But the codes of new life are made of knots of anguish. Always in the stomach, a nauseous feeling. If only one could vomit one's history entirely!

Here, interpreters from different continents and countries coexist. But it is only a false proximity, disconcerting, divergent. Barbed wires between us. No man's lands between us. To know the other would be more dangerous than crossing the borders, seas and oceans. Each one is a world in himself. Each one carries in himself an entire world, a chaotic world. Under the pretence of common traits, the citizens of the global village, together and at the same time so lonely, scatter to infinity. Sometimes we run into each other. Sons of industrialists and sons of village imams, research students and vegetable sellers, Caucasians and Russians, Albanians and Armenians, Indians and Sinhalese, Bengalis and Chakma, Mongolians and Nepalese, Congolese and Chads, Kurds and Arabs, Turks and Arabs, Arabs and Pakistanis, wade in the same tedium, and each waits their turn to begin the gymnastics of languages. Here, the interpreters from mutating and ambitious countries, from orphan and vengeful countries, have vowed together not to become sycophants of the countries from the North. Not to forget. To light a candle at the secret altar of their memory. Memory is a religion. A war. Here, it is the right one. To smash doors, destroy high walls and force entry.

Every day, for several months, I pressed the blue button. I pulled the door even before it opened. I took out my identity card. Never a morning person, I still feigned a smile. The guard used to play a joke on me before extending my identity card. A moment later, the badge reader would read the laminated card and allow me to cross to the other side. Of the ringroad. Of history. Entry into the so-called privileged zones. Later began the nightmarish confusion.

CHERRIES IN THE MOUTH

The earth rotated somehow. Nature changed more spectacularly in the countries from the South than the North. Rivers overflowed. The countries submerged, along with their paddy fields and coconut groves, their thatched huts, their mosques and their temples. And people always went to the safest, the driest of places.

— And you? Were you born here? Did you leave early? Are you mixed-blooded?

The man in charge of interrogation since my arrival at the police station addressed me. I call him Mr K., his last name is long and squawky, I found it hard to remember.

— What is early and what is late? I can spend my life here without belonging to this country.

I instantly regretted speaking those sentences full of ambiguous ideas. I should have simply stated my country of origin, that corresponded to my skin, dark as clay, which resembled the man I assaulted. But, I tell myself, it doesn't take a great deal of insight to spot the differences between him and me, to exactly identify the social classes to which we belonged and to measure the extent to which we differed from one another.

Distracted for a moment, I thought about the panda I had adopted a few months ago. A logo in black relief, smiling, on a brown envelope reassured me that they have collected enough money for green bamboo shoots. I had friends who, at least once in their life, had cleaned beaches where birds had died of petrol ingestion. Engineers, teachers, volunteers for NGOs, worn out by the life that rhythmed to the metro, had become Buddhists. They had always gone to protests where the red vibrant flags flew high like poppies and they chose the blank silence of monasteries once the theories of Hawking became too obscure for their understanding. And during that time, people were still getting deported.

Yesterday, I was in a glass room with lightweight wooden partitions. I found it identical to the semi-opaque, semi-transparent suburban offices where I work. Later, they brought me to this underground room within a parking lot, closed and without any windows. From the shadow rose Mr K., a fragile, pale flame. He had to take my statement. We were seated around a table. The room seemed padded. The uneven concrete layer on the wall was softened awkwardly by a dark blue carpet. Mr K. smiled from the beginning. He apologised many times for the severity of the place. His smile was blond and embarrassed. He was a sweet boy who blushed at the idea of duping others. He beat around the bush. What he wanted to know was not complicated. Seemingly. But seemingly only. I stuttered and sputtered explaining to him why I was here, in this country, and why I had picked the wine bottle and smashed it against the man's skull. At the same time, I observed how funnily Mr K. moved. He went far with his questions, came back, went back again, he demanded justifications, he tried hard to reconstruct the events.

— Was it for love, then? Love for language? Or did you dream about making a living here?

— Love for language, I suppose... As for a job, it came by, over the years...

— Wasn't it a sudden impulse? Not chance? Was it all calculated? Did you know that you would settle down in this country? Did you decide or was it your family?

I did not know how to tell him, but I tried, however, to explain the culmination of a slow project, which had nothing to do with family or professional obligation. I wanted to explain to him my hidden desire, desire born out of long hours spent in the company of books. The amazement. The high. The images of a life lived through a foreign language. To swim and to drown in it.

It was my turn to be on the other side of the invisible computer screen, while Mr. K. took notes on my words and gestures. This role reversal humiliated me. His look, tinted by his increasingly mocking smiles, humiliated me. To save my face, to present a respectable appearance, I began to measure my words as if I was rolling cherries one by one in my mouth before crunching them. I imagined the red drops squirting on to his blond face. It was a year of coincidences. I had changed my role, I had changed positions, creating strange, shadowy figures like in a Chinese play.

We paused at the brink. Between half-secret and half-truth. Between trust and suspicion. He was a sweet boy who blushed at the idea of suspecting others. From then on, he forged ahead. With his invisible scalpel, he wanted to dissect my thoughts. He told me he still did not understand why I had assaulted an unfortunate immigrant, a political asylum seeker. But he forged ahead right to the secret truth hidden deep within me. It had nothing to do with a random act of aggression in public. It had to do with revealing a torturous labyrinth of thoughts, a muddy source of hate, a rage that had suddenly spurted out of a woman of colour taking it out on a man of colour in an attempt to crack his skull.

KALI'S TONGUE

I wake up in the middle of the night and the pain is like boiling oil inside my skull, moving and shifting with each movement that I make. I call the police-man who sleeps seated on a stool in front of the bars. In the bathroom, my head leans toward the floor. The tips of my hair touch and sweep the floor. From its dirty mosaic appear faces and bodies of monsters, beasts, tragic actors, loud-mouths, mourners, grimacers, beastly men, puzzled men, tormented men. They appear at every blink of my eyes, they vanish at every blink.

In my head, I see men incessantly marching, towards the invisible places of the country. It was a year of transgressions, of semi-opaque offices. It was a year of triangles fraught with tension. Between him and me, between him and her, between her and me, between us: asylum seeker, officer and translator. He who begged, she who decided, and me who became a hyphen between them. The words fell like rain. Question marks multiplied on the white screen even before the questions were formulated. I have seen men bite the dust.

I did this work because I loved the gymnastics of languages. I spoke twice as much as anyone else. The officer spoke his language, the language of the host country, the language of the glass-fronted offices. The asylum seeker spoke the language of the supplicant, the language of secrets, the language of the ghetto. And I picked up these sentences, translated them and served them hot. The foreign language melted in my mouth, left its aroma. While I pronounced them, the words of my mother tongue turned clumsily in my mouth, paralysed my tongue, echoed in my head, hammered my brain like the wrong notes of a limp piano. Shuddering between the asylum seekers and me was a frail bridge of hanging rope. I was obliged to lean towards each of these words, extend a hand to them, tilt myself towards these dismembered, dislocated sentences, fish for their disconnected words and collect them, weave them together to form a coherent statement. We spoke the same language, the one we claim as ours. But it was like a cry from my ninth floor to a passer-by on the footpath, to a beggar, crouching and covered in his dirty rags. Even worse, sometimes I felt like I had thrown words of scalding water on their stunned heads. Other times, they pulled themselves together to attack us. When the questions began to put them ill at ease, when they sputtered and it shamed them that they sputtered, when they lied and knew they were lying, when they threw a devious tantrum and screamed that we didn't understand their language. They screamed that I could not translate what they said. They screamed that I did not know their language, that it was not my language.

They had the right to criticise my work, because no woman worthy of her name works. No woman they knew descended so low as to expose herself to the world, to earn a living all alone, as if there were no men left in this world! And certainly no woman dared interrogate them, the men! In the good old days, before all these exploits in seas and offices, when the men cultivated rice and sold spices then returned home without having to show thousands of papers, they would have clouted any woman who dared to snoop on their secrets with her head held high and voice raised. What was absurd was a woman cross-examining them and that they, the men, had to respond to her.

It was at those moments that I could have cracked their skulls. When the misleading words, stinging words, tentacle-like words trapped and wrapped themselves around and stifled my brain. When this chaotic world invaded my body, my territory, and left no more peace inside.

MERCHANTS OF HUMANS

Life is a monologue. Even when we believe we have established a conversation, it is only by chance that two monologues intersect and, perhaps with a little astonishment, stop face to face. In the interview-rooms, questions and answers intersected, but remained isolated. Men were obstinate in their monologue. Women officers threw their arrows of questions almost by habit, weary and aimless. After a few rudimentary interrogations, tension rose between us. The tension rose to a point that sometimes, after the interview ended, everything shook within me and revved up like a parked car whose engine was still on. The man avoided eye contact, I fixed my eyes on him, she bit her lips and anger rose in all of us like nausea. We were riling at each other for nothing. He due to shame, she due to tiredness. I was swaying between shame and irritation.

Because I remembered that I was also from the land of clay, from the eroding land, caught between the teeth of ferocious waters, of the black waters like Kali's tongues, the cruel Goddess who swallowed hectare after hectare. I remembered the mutating cities and the dusty villages, the verdant villages near the forests so dense that sometimes the peasants had to chop off the foliage with an axe to find their way. I remembered the black earth, tender, doughy around the rivers where the tree roots entwined. Children played in the mud, in the water. They caught tiny, agitated fishes, that the waves had brought up to the gently sloping bank. The clay glistened like fishes and mica in the sun, the silvery fishes glittered on the waters up to the invisible line where the bay merged with the low sky.

Urine-coloured yellowed walls of the bathrooms in the police station begin to undulate. The room seems to absorb every beat of my heart, every breath, like a sponge. All the way up to the hallway, nothing moves. The darkness breathes like a sleeping monster.

In this silence, again I hear the incessant footfalls of the men. They are from a land that is detached from the continent, like a diseased limb. They were from a land divided by a political blow. They first invaded the streets and the foot-paths of the neighbouring city of my former subcontinent. Poverty records had been beaten. Living skeletons were being photographed. Teresa, the Mother, the generous one, came to their rescue. But my former subcontinent was not suffi-cient to contain these assaults, to contain these waves of men.

Because, crueller than the politicians, their own land betrayed them. It crumbled into the bay, the water engulfed it. The land played deep-sea diving. Six months under water, six months above to breathe free air. The fields reap-peared like the back of a giant, old turtle.

So, the men wanted to leave. They learnt to swim. They filled their lungs with air and dived into the water. The smugglers guided them to another shore. Corrupt, vicious, wretched *Jungle Book*. From port to port, their brothers waited for them, pocketed the money, helped them embark on boats, on planes. It was a net made of iron. Immigrants were brought there like shining fishes that were transferred from market to market and sold. They are the new millennial slaves. The blacklist stretches as far as the kilometres they have crossed.

Adam-byapari, one of these men said one day. As I translated it to the offi-cer as *merchant of humans*, a blue shiver crept down my back. The merchant of humans had brought this man to this shore too. We found this *Adam-byapari* in other tales. He is the one who has a dozen legal businesses and other hidden ones. He is the one in real estate, tourism, the iron and steel industry. He is the one who served as the middleman for purchasing SIG29, a Russian mil-itary vessel. One of his businesses is to send men to foreign countries, to sell men. Men who are merely slot machines, milk cows; hungry mouths wait for them back in their country. The paltry social aid that they receive in European countries is a windfall to their family. Once sold, contract concluded, these men dispersed and infiltrated the European cities. A Gap jean, a Celio T-shirt, a faux leather jacket did not hide the stench of hunger. It was only a disguise to walk unnoticed among the crowd of this rich city. European dreams, white dreams that the dirty hands, dark hands grabbed as much as they could. The country went up in flames, returned in the night from the nightmares. It had lost everything, soul and body, blood and breath. It became an idea of what it was. It did not exist any more.

And always, always the migrating men, going more and more to the north from the south, while the north of their country, the north of the nearest frontier did not satisfy them any more, did not welcome them any more, they crossed the red lines, searched the far north, the north of the dream, they entered the place where they do not have the right. The tension increased in the room. The words could not convince anyone. The men sweated, stuttered, crossed and uncrossed their fingers, repeated the questions as if they were the answers, recited sentences in silence, their Adam's apples bobbed up and down, the words gurgled in their voice, tumbled out, pale and frightened. Words were added to words. Files stacked one on top of the other. Men paraded without an end in sight. One couldn't differentiate their face or their body. Together like a gigantic dark heap, they put us ill at ease. They were forced to lie, to tell a story different from their own to try to seek political asylum. They shouldered the burden of a life that was completely foreign to them. They tried to slide into the skin of characters created by the merchants of humans, their own compatriots. Obviously, one almost never believed their stories. Bought along with the journey and passport, they yellowed and fell apart with so many other stories accumulated over the years.

Long after I left the offices, the words returned to me in the bare room at night. Their confused noise filled it, overflowed in it. Some nights I woke up breathless, as if I was submerged in the rising tide of whispers, murmurs and cries. In my half-sleep, I saw their faces and bodies sprouting out of the mosaic floor. The men, dumbstruck, puzzled, tormented. They appeared at every blink of my eye. They vanished at every blink of my eye. Like this night, in this cell at the police station. At the end of the day, I am still not cured of their cries and whispers.

THE CLAY LAND

— I want to take you to the place you left, from where you fled, said Mr K., during the first interrogation.
— I can't go back to the place I left. It's not there any more.
— What's not there any more?
— The place.
— What do you mean?
— The space has moved with time. It's the impossible geometry of life.
— ...

— It's like the stars the sailors see. With every onslaught of the waves, they are pushed farther away. Their stars shift. Place and time travel. Point of origin, the port and its boats, this space is buried deep in the memory. It's nowhere else. It'll never come back. The knots are undone.

— Do you ever regret? Does the choice that you made seem fair to you?

— ... What's to regret?

I recounted the memory of an afternoon by the river to him. It was one of those autumnal days where one could dip one's fingers in the light as if it were honey. I had just arrived in this country. Everything that I tasted seemed so delicious, despite the messiness of administrative paperwork. I was sitting at the edge of the river, face to the sun, across from the green boxes of bookstores on the other bank that waited patiently like infinite frogs in a fairy tale. My legs hung over the water that flowed languidly. I expected no interruption on this day, until a voice called out from afar, from the opposite quay. It was so exact, a line so straight and candid, from one bank to another, that I couldn't have mistaken it: 'Miss! Miss!' 'Yes?' I shouted back, and I saw two different silhouettes. Two men. A young boy, very young, barely an adolescent, and the other one less young, more like an uncle who had brought him for a walk, a day in the sun. 'You aren't going to jump in the water, are you?' The concern in his voice reached me despite the wind and the distance. 'Of course not! Not today,' I responded, and our smiles fluttered beyond the waves.

— It's always like this with the people here: I am facing their river, their life, so close to them but in the wrong direction. Yet they understand me, they address me with a cheery sympathy, with the tender concern that one would have for a puppy.

Mr K.'s eyes wandered for a moment, then as if to conclude, settled on me.

— Ever get nostalgic? Homesick?

I stopped rocking my chair. My feet were placed unmoving on the ground. As if nailed with disgrace. The memory made me look at the floor, at the dark knots of my past. I wanted to drag Mr K. with me there. With a sly pleasure, I wanted to see him affected, stirred with emotion, unsettled.

Homesick? It was the country that was sick. Memory of the ancestors. Grandma's tale. Old money passed down from one generation to the next. I passed it now to Mr K. Remembrance of the other side. *Opar Bangla.* I described to him how the men, a little before the bloody days of independence, had fled the country. Like nobly bred dogs, they had smelt danger. They had fled the clash between the separatists and the strong colonists from their police and their army.

Memory had to be invented. Thanks to the stench of blood and gun powder. I spoke to him about explosions of railways, telegraph poles, police stations. The men who shot at the white officers while they got off their cars had to be imagined. It seemed that they sometimes shot badly. Wives and daughters of the officers, in evening gowns, an adolescent boy, his tennis racket in hand, all collapsed together in a pool of blood, soon attracting late winter flies.

Memory also had to be taught. School textbooks explained how the authorities had searched for ways to divide the region, based on the separatist movements. How, at the beginning of the previous century, militants had succeeded in annulling the divisions of regions, and how, forty years later, during independence, when each side tried to reap benefits, the country, a single body, was mutilated. How this fertile land was pilfered, humiliated, persecuted, and finally chopped into two, quartered by the colonial cavalry.

Fairy tales made way to fiery tales. Many years later, while the rain beat down on the wooden window shutters, while the lanterns swayed and when the giant shadows danced on the walls, the shouts of *Allah ho Akbar* and *Jay Hind* launched by the two religious camps, Hindus and Muslims, could be heard: the clash began again every night. Monsters and demons from stories had given way to these fanatics that stampeded one over the other on the streets with axes, knives, switchblades, sticks and guns. They said that the men fell like banana trees. They also said that the police force of Surabardi had finally decided to declare a state of emergency when the rioters' guns had run out of bullets and when the switchblades remained planted in the chopped bodies. Peace came unsteadily, with its vulture wings, dark, stifling, peace with the stench of death, dumb and dazed with shame. The switchblade not only rips the skin, but it also reveals the ugliness residing in us, the flesh opens and unfolds itself in front of our eyes, more forbidden than before, the frenzy begins, time stops. To kill is intoxicating. One cannot go back on it. The corpses accumulate in the memory. Insurmountable piling. Once the logic of death is established and practised, peace seems unreal. How does one justify the silence when violence and commotion have taken its place? Only fatigue slowed these men. After independence, after the Partition, during the days and weeks, the men went to the other side of the border by foot, their whole life tied into a tight bundle, their entire lives suddenly cut at the roots. City footpaths overflowed with corpses and bodies that still stirred, that begged, pleaded for water, for rice water, starchy water that is thrown away after cooking rice, they dared not ask for more. From their abandoned kitchens, from the other side of the barbed wires, the smoke from the blazes still rose. The partition line sometimes travelled through houses, kitchen in one country, bedrooms in another. Obviously, an absurd division, however well-calculated. Harvest fields in one country, factories in another. Poverty programmed for decades. From then on, the men have not stopped migrating. Crossing lines. Going beyond the red line. Entering where they don't have the right.

Heat rose from the ground. It burnt the soles of my feet. As hot as the rice water that grandma gave to the lifeless lying on the footpaths.

It was strange, all the same! To not ask any more. How does one beg? How does one raise the first cry? How does one cry to beg for rubbish? Who can go back, get back on one's feet, become the man again after having swallowed garbage fighting it off the stray dogs?

But this conversation deviated and returned to the heart of the matter.

Instead of taking me to the place I fled, my birth country, Mr K. asked me more about the nature of my work. If I kept my eyes open. If I had my ears erect. Or even, if I was impartial in my role. If I carried my mask well. If I had suffocated under this mask. If I had ever wanted to tear everything apart, to throw in the towel and howl.

But Mr K. wanted to cast doubt, the fog, the leeway of chameleon words. Words, open to mean everything and nothing.

'Do you think that you were patient enough with these asylum seekers? Would you have had the same air of anger and violence if it had been a man from this country?' He cleared his throat and then added: 'A European, I mean.'

A White, you mean, I gnaw at these words inside.

His suspicions hardly touched me. He erased them with an indulgent smile. As if it were nothing. As if I had not assaulted the man, as if I had not been put under interrogation. Then, he backtracked. Not finishing his sentences, he waited for me to respond with one badly chosen word, one word that would make me fall into his trap.

We advanced and retreated behind the mirrors erected out of words, as if in an ancient theatre performance where no one dared to break them. It was a poor operetta. Without a real ambition.

I was thinking about another plot, a more secretive one, one that was more strained. And it was so delicate that it would not exist if I had not thought of it. Between Lucia and me. Lucia was all fire, all ice. As an officer, she was fearsome. All she lacked was a whip and thigh-high boots. She lashed at the men, assured them that it was for their own good, that it was necessary to tell the truth, that it was the only way she could help them. Then, she would look at me. And it was impossible for me to meet her gaze. The blue of her eyes was exasperatingly beautiful. A grey-blue stone, semi-liquid, small imperceptible bands of a wheel. With a glow that I guessed was white. I guessed because I have never looked at Lucia for more than half a second. My head barely turned towards her, I lowered my eyes. And much later, now, alone or with my colleagues, in the crowd, hurtling down the streets, this glow came back to me, like a promise and of forbidden things. Maybe I assaulted the man because of Lucia. All these men make me feel ashamed. And without knowing it, I yielded more and more to these women officers who represented law, righteousness and authority. I was on the other side. I was leaning with my heart heavy toward those women who had been exhausted by the endless parade of the men seeking asylum.

Anaemic, thin and nervous, these women. And my politically incorrect tenderness. Maybe I assaulted the man because in front of Lucia and other officers, in front of us women, the man and his kind was almost an insult, an error, an accident. To my eyes, their misery did not justify their incompetence and lies, their aggression and meanness. I stuttered, first of all, in front of Mr K. Then, my voice gained strength little by little and I felt free and entitled for a moment.

— You think that you have the right to correct a supposedly false system all by yourself? Mr K. questioned me.

I did not reply. I lowered my head. I thought of everything that remained motionless. The footpaths are still as dry and cracked as ever. Beggars, prostitutes and day workers talk in their sleep. A dog barks in the distance. The heavy screen of the night does not move. From afar, I see them. From afar, I look at my country with envy as it goes on all these years without me. These years of pleasure and abundance. These years of disappointment and masquerade. The slumdog from the ghetto wins the jackpot and the ghetto remains a ghetto.

City employees bulldoze the huts. Fathers sell their daughters. Girls enter the wide-open mouths of the metropolises. Child soldiers sort garbage, serve tea, hammer iron, stop cars at traffic signals and wipe the windows, weasel themselves to seats higher than their head, do shopping and clean vessels at rich people's homes, break the chandeliers and the statues whose beauty they failed to understand, sell vegetables and steal when they can, the grocers throw them out, they return to the village, to the footpath, to the hut where they were born.

They return to the jaws of the devil. Child soldiers protect their home with their matchstick arms. They fill their bony cage with deep breath and plunge into the dirty pool of rain, in the large holes in the footpaths. The river overflows and drowns the city.

The men too. When the rain and mud devour their lands, they try to run as fast as the water. The sand covers the rice fields. The men go to faraway countries. On a foggy sky, they see new lines of horizon rising.

But the laws remain unchanged. Tectonic plates slide under tectonic plates. The canvas of the sky is perforated like an old circus tent. Entire countries collapse in water, a grim future. And still, hordes of men climb up to the north. With their lies, their meanness, their incompetent obstinacy, their sad, rag-like dreams.

The immigrants survive despite everything, like rebel stems pushing through a barren land. They find ways to avoid blows from the sickle.

Nothing is lost, nothing is created, everything transforms into images and dreams and nightmares. The night thickens in my cell like ink at the bottom of the inkwell before the first light of the day. The milky dawn soothes the cell in slats. Carnivorous plants twist their necks here and there in the darkness. I have a ball in my throat. Vomiting is the only way it will get out. Crying has the effect of alcohol. It intoxicates. It empties and makes you want to vomit. I don't like crying for others.

ELAD LASSRY   INTERVIEW

On my way to meet Elad Lassry, a Lyft driver tells me about his wife. 'She had liver cancer. I helped her heal it, holistically. Then we learnt how to reverse ageing.' It is 10 a.m. on a Sunday morning. We are in Los Angeles, speeding towards Melrose Avenue, West Hollywood, where the photographer, filmmaker and sculptor lives. Since 2007, Lassry has been making work that deconstructs and destabilises image systems, building a bank of 'units' – images of lipstick, landscapes, cats or men, which appear to be generic. Most have been shot in Lassry's studio, and examine conventions of catalogue photography, courting vacancy and unease. Many show perfect faces, model animals, unblemished fruit – seductive images that might be described as kitsch. These pictures are shown alongside found images: negatives taken from magazine archives, say, which are never credited.

Born in Tel Aviv, Lassry moved to California in 1998 to enrol at California Institute of the Arts (CalArts). Later, he took a graduate programme at the University of Southern California, where he produced a series of work in 2007 that made him famous. Over the past ten years, his practice has evolved in exhibitions, all titled 'Elad Lassry', which show images that are neither pictures nor objects, but something in between – shown in brightly coloured box frames, hidden behind silk curtains, or with objects affixed to the picture. In his latest series, *Untitled (Assignment)* (2018 – 19), Lassry hired models to shoot an imaginary fashion campaign, seen applying make-up, photographing each other against an almost blank grey backdrop, or holding familiar poses. (One of these images, featuring the 22-year-old model Jean Campbell, appears on the cover of *The White Review*.)

When my cab pulls up to Lassry's avenue, I see rows of white picket fences, kitschy gnomes and fake lawns under a crisp blue sky. Lassry answers the door, it shakes and scratches open and I step right into his kitchen. Unlike the portraits I've seen of him crouching in a vest and bandana, looking mean, the man I meet appears a little shy. He apologises for the apparent mess, a room scattered with children's toys. His Apple Mac is Sellotaped to the tabletop. On his neck I notice a tattoo of a poodle, and the name 'JESSICA' inked in sloping caps. We sip filtered water and pick dried fruit from a small wooden bowl. He appears at once defensive and kind.

Over the course of our two-hour conversation, there will be many distractions. Jessica, the commemorated poodle, pads into the kitchen now and then, and Lassry jumps to attend to her needs. The shopping arrives – paper bags of vegetables, muesli, pots of yoghurt – which Lassry unpacks while we talk. He is restless, perhaps agitated, and our conversation swings between what feels like theoretical sparring – debating indexicality, photography as a haunted medium, the fragility of images – and moments of personal revelation. He compliments my clothes, shares personable anecdotes, lets me pet his dog, but at the same time, he also acts as an adversary – contradicting me, detailing his point, before rounding back, a little later, to agree. His practice, Lassry explains, is often misunderstood. A point of frustration is the popular interpretation of his 2007 series – the images of cats and lipstick in coloured frames, which are dominant when encountering Lassry online, and which appeal to kitschiness, although Lassry contends they are not to be read as such. As in all his images, Lassry tries to keep the viewer conscious of the systems through which the meaning of every picture is refracted.   IZABELLA SCOTT

THE WHITE REVIEW   I read that you have a dog called Julia Kristeva.

ELAD LASSRY   I did. Her full name was Tuna Julia Kristeva. I got her on discount at the Beverly Center in a pet store that's now shut down. She died at 14. Did you read about how Julia Kristeva was a spy – a Bulgarian spy in Paris? She denies it, but I suspect that she was. You know, when I was younger I didn't really think of LA. Having grown up in Tel Aviv, the cultural centre was Europe – specifically London. I applied to The Slade [School of Fine Arts, London] in the late 1990s after high school and got rejected, so I researched other places and that led me to California. OMG, everyone is so good-looking in London. But I usually only talk about my work. My life is not necessarily something I carry into my work.

TWR   Why don't we begin with your early work. You reconfigure existing, popular images – some are actual stock photographs, others you meticulously stage. Melons, wigs, Anthony Perkins, lipstick, shoes. Cats, wolves, zebras, flamingos. I've never really heard you say exactly where the found images come from – how do you collect?

EL   For some reason, my early work comes up more than my recent work in academic essays or interviews and whatnot. This work was very much a series of singular, stripped-down subjects and objects: the man, the woman, the animal, the landscape, and so on. But there's a suggestion that none is quite functioning as they propose to. Take the cat in a blue frame [*Russian Blue* (2012)]. The status of the cat is not clear. Is it a stock image for a calendar? Is it alive or stuffed? Is it part of a genre, i.e. cat photography? I approached the work with equal attention to image and object, presenting images in box-frames that very much had a presence, and these frames in many ways challenged the experience of the picture. The viewer was encouraged to wonder what makes the picture more of an image than an object, or why what is inside the box might have more presence than the box itself. You asked about how I came to collect these images, but I'm not interested in collecting. Neither am I interested in making good or beautiful images. In terms of my practice, there is no mood, there is no inspiration. It has always been very much a case of facilitating my interest in the history of pictures, and of figuring out some rather philosophical and open-ended questions about what representation is, and how it functions. And that interest has been articulated in collecting, or I would say producing, pictures in which representation had failed in some way, or where the space of representation was curious. I'm interested in studying instances where the picture does not quite deliver its promise. I am always asking: what do pictures mean?

TWR   You seem to move through genres, cataloguing visual styles – product photography, portraiture, animal photography, to name a few. Are you discovering what pictures mean by identifying types?

EL   I'm thinking about systems, and how integral systems are to how we understand pictures. Images are dependent on multiple histories, agencies, standards and conventions. My early work presents a bank of pictures involved in multiple systems – from textbooks, 'how-to' guides, typologies and so on. This bank might show anything from dentistry photography to pictures from perfect pregnancy books. The purpose of these pictures is not purely photographic; they are used to illustrate something, or show how something is done, and that is what people call 'stock-like' or 'advertising-like'. I approach these qualities as built in; I'm not looking to necessarily expose this dependence I'm speaking of, but I assume it is an almost dormant visual. But as well as being caught within a system, the images also have a life outside the system. The photograph showing dental fillings was taken to illustrate an academic lecture, but it is a visually dense image too; it claims a sort of independence that the system cannot control. Pictures can never be completely autonomous, but in my work I claim a sense of autonomy.

TWR   How? In the way you frame them, making the photographs also sculptural?

EL   The images are boxed-off, hermetically sealed, and exude a sense of being fixed or finished. They could make a claim of three-dimensionality. I want them to seem ready to be shipped, produced in a size that is manageable for travel – and in a way, they take part in the history of the postcard, because there's a mobility that is inherent to pictures. A popular thing to say nowadays is that it's easy to send a photograph – but it has always been easy. But what I'm saying is that, on the one hand, these early images are familiar or comforting or corny, because the content is so generic and stock-like that we feel we've seen it so many times: *that* kind of girl, *that* kind of cat. And at the same

time, in terms of the making, the images are sealed, inaccessible, autonomous.

TWR   This tension within the images might be understood as a kind of duplicity. That's one definition of irony: saying one thing, and meaning another. Perhaps your images relate to irony in the purest sense?

EL   I'm trying to show that there is something very elastic inside the picture's finished unit. It's important that the images look final and too-general at once. They lack a lot of information, which I think makes them troubling – for example, you mentioned Anthony Perkins. His portrait often appears in my work and, like every other image, is never credited. There's often a sense of manufacture behind these images – an economy that you might sense, but cannot quite pinpoint or comprehend. Most of the images of Perkins which have ended up in my work are ones of his early days in Hollywood [in the 1950s], which happens to be a very specific decade in regards to homosexuality. The studios were known to arrange dates for gay men in an effort to maintain the possibility of stardom, and the economic capacity to carry a feature. Indeed, Perkins landed a contract for a series of films in which he starred opposite a female love interest. But in almost all of these films, he failed to deliver what is conceived as an archetype of a typical man. In more than a handful, there's a silent queerness written into the script, I think – in stories of a man stricken with mental trauma; an estranged son; a young sheriff in need

of guidance from an experienced man. In 1960, after a decade of awkward performances, Perkins managed to depart from this stable Hollywood role in Hitchcock's Lacanian nightmare, *Psycho*. [He played Norman Bates.] *Psycho* seems to stabilise Perkins's 'picture'; in it, he makes sense for the first time (and indeed, he proceeded to pursue more and more sequels, *Psycho II-IV*). In the 1970s, Perkins made efforts to curb his outsider status through marriage to a woman and the making of a family, only to have that structure burst by the media outing of his HIV-positive status in 1990.

All this history isn't in my work; it doesn't have to be. What is in the work is a ghost of that history. It's a dormant yet crucial quality of the work: a man's oscillating identity, locked in an image which has a structure of its own. Some years ago, I obtained the negatives of an editorial Perkins initiated for *People* magazine in his very final days [in 1992], in which he essentially performed a perfect family day at his house in the Hollywood Hills. The photographs show Perkins and his wife in the kitchen preparing food; Perkins and his two sons playing basketball in the backyard. Frail and AIDS-stricken, Perkins is fighting another giant structure: a hostile media. This publicity shoot was an attempt to assure the public that Perkins was still a next-door-neighbour, a nice, heterosexual man; that AIDS and his homosexuality were simply a hateful rumour. He died the same year. My interest is in the suspension of the image; they appear to be occasions where something outside the picture is fighting against the visual information presented.

'Ironic' is a word I resort to when describing my work to people who are not invested in art. I meet somebody at the gym, and when they see my work, and they say, 'Oh, it's ironic', I say 'Yes', otherwise they will think I am actually making work about a man smiling. Does it really mean that the work is ironic? No. But it's a good start to find it curious, to think it's not as it seems. It's a first step. The cat in the blue frame is not ironic, but the cat is many other things. Every photograph has a set of relations behind it. In this case, the genre of cat photography has, for many years, been fetishised as a source of mass comfort. When my practice is looked up online, people see cats and lipstick. Either they laugh or they say: 'I love your work, I love the cats and lipstick.' I say thank you.

TWR   I'm interested in your idea about the images being 'too-finished'. For me, they tip over into something scopophilic, where looking is almost erotic. This also relates to some of your later work, photographs that are half obscured by pleats of silk affixed to the frame, shown at your first exhibition at 303 Gallery in 2013. Is this a kind of visual tease?
EL   For me, these works are too finished and too perfect to be erotic; they have a shine, or gloss, which is alienating. When I shoot images that appear to people as stock photographs, I consistently use a very high focal stop, which brings all of the photo into focus. It's an untraditional way to photograph products. Stock photographs would ideally illustrate something and serve that object – i.e., choose it as the subject. My method of putting everything in focus is a subtle means of reassessing the status of the subject within a photograph.

I'm actually not interested in photography. Often people, curators and such, confuse my work as being about photography, or about making photographs according to whatever set of conventions currently define a good photograph. My work does unfold mainly as photography-based, but the question of representation goes far beyond the medium of photography. I think it's difficult for people to accept photography as a means to an end – simply as a tool to make work – because it is so overwhelmingly *there*, and so seemingly accurate.
TWR   That's part of photography's fascinating contradiction – that it is so much like the world we see, so close to our experience of vision, but at the same time, is absolutely nothing like it: warped, flattened, framed.
EL   My photographs seem to be viewed mostly online, where their existence must seem very photographic. However, physically I am presenting objects that carry an image. I suspect that when seen in-person their photographic qualities somehow vanish. I print on glossy paper – I was printing on glossy paper in the early 2000s when it was considered very unsophisticated; matte was taken more seriously. I was also intentionally using reflective glass – I mean, who uses reflective glass, rather than museum glass? But I was *choosing* the reflection. And these choices give the photographs an eeriness, because they are trapped between a sense of confidence – being very finished and absolute – and also shakiness – a sense that the whole illusion of meaning can easily fall apart.

With the earlier work, I would get frustrated that the most glossy, colourful images were the most popular, and that people didn't seem to access the larger structure. Really smart people would say, 'You're a colourist.' I disagree. When I paint a frame, I choose the worst colour I can think of. But the nature of colour is that it's always beautiful. I don't think you can have a bad colour. I'm a surgeon more than a colourist. The works are not meant to be pretty, and yet they appear to many people as pretty photographs. To really see them, the photographs demand that viewers get over the fact that they are 'well-made'. But people get stuck, especially on images that take part in visuals that communicate some kind of promotional quality. Advertising overwhelms most other visual cues, after all, it's targeted.

TWR   It's interesting that you ended up making these very seductive images, without that being your intent.
EL   Mark-making is seductive – it comes from a genealogy of representing the sublime. But what I'm interested in is art that activates ideas. Perhaps this art is overwhelmingly beautiful, perhaps it's not, but either way, beauty is not at the core of the work. The endgame for me is an art experience – this quality that we have, as humans, of further understanding and reflecting on the nature of being.

TWR   Is beauty a distraction?
EL   On the contrary, I think that beauty serves the work really well conceptually – as a visual trap

to make the work easy to engage with, and so on.
I often look back to my first museum show in 2010,
curated by Beatrix Ruf at Kunsthalle Zurich, as an
exhibition that tapped into that quality. If you look
at the installation shots, you see that the beauty of
the images – and I'm not apologising for their beau-
ty – is curbed by other factors. First, the images are
absurdly small. People don't realise this until they
see them in a gallery. And then there's the exhibi-
tion layout. What the images are shown next to is
crucial. An image is never autonomous; it's always
hijacked by what is next to it. A picture of a girl
followed by a picture of a dog creates a picture in
the middle of a girl and a dog. I make sure to hang
images that work against each other.

When you enter the gallery space, all you
would see is a row of consecutive coloured lines –
the frames. I wanted the exhibition to feel clinical,
systematic, harsh, and to create a sense of distance,
or alienation. These image-objects also reference
a very particular economy, in that each one is
standard Kodak size, the available size, 36 × 28 cm,
the size of a magazine page.

When I started at CalArts in 1998, photo-
graphs were enormous. Photography at the time
was trying to take on painting – trying to take on
that space of the monumental. Gregory Crewdson
was heading a popular photography programme at
Yale where giant prints of enigmatic scenarios were
abundant. Sharon Lockhart, who was one of my
teachers at CalArts, thought about photography
and narrative, where photography was a conversa-
tion between what happened before, and after.

TWR   And your very small images pushed
against this?
EL   My prints were only slightly bigger than
a negative, like contact sheets. They ranged from
exotic fruits to domestic dogs, yet there was
something questionable about them. They had the
quality of a stock photograph, but then again, as
I mentioned before, they were not quite like stock
photos. Both general yet specific, I think they trig-
gered questions of provenance and selection. I was
interested in toying with different histories: from
experimental and Bauhaus photography to 1950s
catalogue images, or images that were peculiar, like
something from a Colgate commercial. Why were
they in a group? When you entered the show at
Kunsthalle Zurich, only as you started walking did
the exhibition unfold. I liked this quality – a kind
of analogue unfolding, as if the coloured lines were
digital files.

TWR   You know exactly how you want your
work to be seen, viewed and read. Is it possible to
control this?
EL   Some subjects fight for their presence harder
than others. People, for example, are more domi-
nant subjects than balloons. There's a hierarchy, but
one that in my work is not photographic – because
the images are shot with the same camera, printed
the same size, mounted in the same frame. The
hierarchy has to do with knowledge, power and the
history of photography. For me, there is something
vacant about all images. They are photos of some-
thing and nothing at the same time. The photo

of the Hollywood lake, *90068* (2010), and the photograph of the papayas, *Tropical Fruits* (2007), are in many ways the same photograph. The work has never been about what's in it. The only thing that keeps a photograph from completely evaporating, conceptually speaking, is its indexicality. It is an index of a moment in time. This is the only currency a photograph has. The images have been called 'irritating' or annoying – that's what Beatrix Ruf called them in her catalogue essay. I love that she said that. It's a great way to describe the images. And perhaps all photographs are irritating because we know there are many of them, but we only see one. I think of photographs as having no author at all. I've never been interested in which photos I make, and which I've found. The very nature of the medium is multiplicity, a negative that can be printed endlessly.

TWR   When I look at your work, despite what you have said, I still see it as kitsch. Not kitsch in the way Walter Benjamin famously described it in 'Dream Kitsch' (1925) – something cosy and familiar, void of criticality – but a staged and refined iteration of it.
EL   I've never been comfortable with the word kitsch. It has a sense of comfort that my work doesn't retain. I think there's something very harsh about photographs. There is a perversion, to quote Jennifer Blessing, the Guggenheim curator – a perversion in the sense of how these images sneak back on you, right after you've processed them. I think she meant perversion in the sense of the shift of something from its original course, to a distortion of what was first intended. When I develop a picture, I often find myself intrigued by slippages of function, utility or presence. I resort to a kind of alteration (i.e. perversion) which seems to participate in this misplacement – such as when a bird or animal oscillates between a merely decorative pattern and an elevated subject (facing the camera, carefully focused, composed), as in *Eagle Glove, Falcon (Kodak)* (2008).
    Maybe our definitions of kitsch are different. I don't think the work of Jeff Koons is kitsch, for example. Other people do. To me, kitsch has a fuzziness to it. Kitsch could never reveal so much violence. My own work is optically sharp – pornographic is a better word – in its harshness. The photographs kind of freak me out at times – there is so much missing that they create a sense of lack, yet what is there is fucking aggressive.

TWR   You mentioned earlier how important it was for you that the work is seen in person. Is an exhibition the most important thing?
EL   I think in terms of the white cube. I would like to say that I'm somebody making work that could be seen anywhere, but it's just not true. My work gets activated by something very traditional, the blankness of the exhibition space. When I exhibit work, everything is controlled and calculated: the distance between photographs, the size, the repetitions.

TWR   A counterpart to your 2018 show at frac île-de-france in Paris is now opening at Sommer Contemporary Art, Tel Aviv as 'Elad Lassry' (2019). Can you tell me about the show?
EL   I shot the first set, *Untitled (Assignment)* (2018) [one of which appears on the cover of *The White Review*], in a studio using working models, so some faces are slightly familiar. I conceptualised it as a self-commissioned assignment, an unsolicited campaign. My interest was in a starting point that was cancelled in many ways: an assignment that was not assigned. I followed some silent, predetermined rules in making these images, conventions of standard catalogue photography. I was also asking models to participate in a fully pre-determined convention, and work from an industry position. It was essential, when working with Jean Campbell for example [who appears on the cover of *The White Review*], to know that she was booked for a similar commercial assignment. The photographs on display are so similar to each other that they start to empty of meaning. There is no clear reason for why they exist, or why they are here in a museum. The vacancy in them is aggressive in relation to the museum's space. They are low status, exchangeable images, serving what used to be editorial – like how *Vogue* might go back to a photo from five years ago about lipstick, because they have a new article about lipstick. So the photographs are available and exchangeable and also somehow pre-existing, put to use for so many purposes.
    That's one set of images. In another room are photographs from a second unsolicited assignment, this time more journalistic – photographs of a facility that packages corals. Here, my approach was very straightforward. There is nothing about these images that couldn't illustrate a *New York Times* article about the coral depot. Indeed, the whole exhibition is about making properly utilitarian photographs.

I read an essay by François Laruelle, 'The Concept of Non-Photography' (2011). He writes that in many ways the only thing a photograph is like is another photograph. It's such a beautiful, radical idea – that a photograph can't be anything else but like another photograph. This speaks so much to what I'm doing. I'm making photographs that openly have no status within a modern consideration of a photograph. If the earlier photographs were a visual trap, defeating themselves at their own game, this time it's impossible to fall into the same trap. There's no way.

TWR   It sounds like a brave move. The seductiveness of the early photographs was part of what makes them popular; anyone can like them. Whereas these are much harder.
EL   I don't find one series harder than the other. To my mind, photography has always been a difficult medium, with its history of interventions and manipulations. For example, famously, the genre of ghost photography in the Victorian era. People believed you could photograph a dead relative floating above your head. But it was just early Photoshop tricks – sandwiching negatives, or maybe you retouched the negative to make somebody appear a certain way. If photographs don't make it harder to look, then we forget these histories.

You know, I often realise that for many people, the experience of art is not focused in philosophy and the experience of being, but rather is about beauty. In terms of photography, beauty is hard to look past, and that's where some people end. A beautiful flower is a beautiful flower. People say to me, 'What's your inspiration? Who's your favourite artist?' There are so many preconditions to popular understandings of art. These people want me to look like an artist. They wonder where the paint-splattered trousers are. They ask me, 'Do you use oil?'

TWR   The romantic myth of the artist?
EL   I dislike popular understandings of art. Recently, somebody tried to set me up with a guy, it was a funny date. The guy was cute, nice, and he'd recently got into yoga. At some point the conversation turned to art; I asked, 'What kind of art do you like?' And he said, 'That's a tough question because everything is art. Trees are art. The desert is art. The ocean is art.' I find this viewpoint challenging. This way of thinking is a real misunderstanding and a dismissal of the human mind. Trees, deserts, oceans are phenomena. That doesn't mean they're art. To say so is completely dismissing the human experience. Art is the decision.

I. S.,
March 2019

WORKS

PLATES

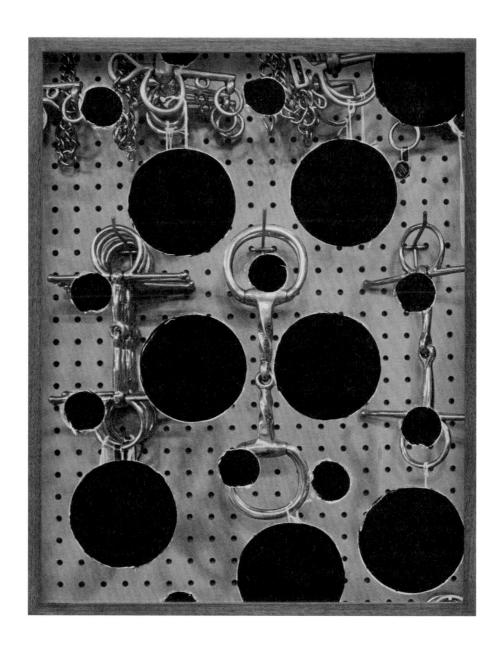

XVIII

XXIII

SELECTED ANNAHS
KHAIRANI BAROKKA

An opera singer, Mme Nina Pack, was on friendly terms with a rich banker who had business relations with the traders of the Malayan Isles. The singer happened to say before the representative of one of these, 'I would like to have a little negro girl.' A few months later a policeman brought Mme Nina Pack a young, half-breed, half-Indian, half-Malayan, who had been found wandering about the Gare de Lyon. She had a label hung around her neck, with the inscription: *Mme Nina Pack, rue de la Rochefoucauld, à Paris. Envoi de Java.* She was given the name of Anna. Some time later, in consequence of a little domestic drama in which Anna was implicated, she was dismissed. She came to me, as I had known her at her employer's house, to ask me to find her a good situation. I judged her qualifications as a housemaid to be very middling, and thought she stood more chance of succeeding as a model. I told Gauguin about her.

'Send her to me. I'll try her,' he said.

Anna pleased him, and he kept her.

—Ambroise Vollard (Gauguin's art dealer), 1936

The title of Paul Gauguin's 1893-94 portrait *Annah La Javanaise. Aita tamari vahine Judith te parari* has two parts, describing its subject in two different languages: literally, 'Annah the Javanese [in French]. The child-woman (sometimes child-girl) Judith has not been breached [in Tahitian]'. Relatively little is known of the real young person or people who inspired the painting. The instances in which people – whether art historians, the Nobel laureate Mario Vargas Llosa, or writers of art institution copy – have written of Annah contradict each other often, offering up vague and conflicting details of a supposedly insignificant life. Annah's ethnicity shifts, her origin ranges from 'streets' to 'brothels'; I have seen the exact same picture of a girl labelled 'Annah La Javanaise' also labelled as 'Teha'amana', a Polynesian teenager who'd been married to Gauguin. There is so much variation in accounts of her life that it's plausible multiple brown children could have been mistaken for one. For that matter, it's possible that Annah was trans or of a non-Western gender, though presenting as a girl (and thus possibly desirous of 'they' as their pronoun in English). These children exist in the archives as an afterthought, an appendage to a coterie of white, European, male painters in late-nineteenth century France, primarily Paul Gauguin.

I first learned of *Annah La Javanaise* in 2011. Today it is held in a private collection, inaccessible to the general public except when loaned out to museum exhibitions. I discovered its existence online, and thus experienced it, as most people now do, as a series of pixels on a screen, a digital ghost of an artwork whose original form exists exclusively for its wealthy owners. My first thought upon seeing the picture was that it showed a Javanese girl like myself; a body presenting and labelled as a Javanese woman – though in photographs in the Gauguin archives, a similar-looking girl certainly presents as a child – documented abroad in the nineteenth century, captured in both painted and photographic form. This is rare to see. At that time, I had begun to think increasingly about women's pain, being in acute and untreated pain myself for what would later be diagnosed as nerve damage. It was this experience that drew me to Annah. The figure – figures – of Annah crystallised ideas that had been on my mind: the link between chronic pain and historical abuse; the way women are less likely to be believed when they experience pain, by the medical establishment and/or friends and family; the compounding of women's pain due to that disbelief, and the compounding of this disbelief due to gender and race.

Since my discovery of the painting eight years ago, I have held onto Annah dearly as a composite of figures to whom I could relate. Their probable horrors and experiences are different from mine, but here was a labelled-Javanese girl who could well have been in pain, but for whom the possibility of pain does not occur to an ablenormative world. In subsequent years, I have projected scenarios of their escape and self-fulfilment onto my fiction, poetry and visual art, knowing that in reality, a child in their circumstances at that time was very likely to have suffered throughout their life. After all, presenting as young, brown girls in 1890s France, they would have lived lives of isolation, and their guardian Gauguin was a known domestic abuser who would certainly today be classified as a sexual predator. Gauguin delighted in humiliating all women, but targeted women descended from European colonies precisely because they were less protected. In *Noa Noa*, the journal of his time in Tahiti, Gauguin reminisced, 'I saw plenty of calm-eyed young women, I wanted them to be willing to be taken without a word: taken brutally. In a way longing to rape.'

Gauguin lived in what was then French Polynesia twice, first from 1891 to 1893 – when he was in charge of an official mission from the French Ministry of Education and Culture – and again from 1895 until his death in 1903. During his first trip to Tahiti, he reportedly took three brides, aged between thirteen and fourteen, and was rumoured to have given them and others syphilis. Yet the artistic result of Gauguin's Polynesian trips – his famed portraits of brown girls – are not seen as artefacts of abuse but as remarkable contributions to Western art history. In 1896, Gauguin was commissioned to paint a portrait of Vaite Goupil, the nine-year-old daughter of his Tahiti-based French patron Auguste Goupil. The disturbingly adult nature of the portrait may have been what caused Goupil to distance himself from Gauguin, yet there was no known outcry from patrons about Gauguin's use of brown girls as sexual objects. In Paris and Brittany, between trips to Tahiti, he was seen in the company of Annah – it's been assumed she was sexually involved with him, though even the fact that she ever posed nude for him is an assumption, and cannot be proven.

Over time, my understanding of who the children labelled as Annah might be has expanded, as I've investigated the role of ableism as combined with white supremacy in arts institutions. I've grown increasingly aware of the ways in which archival texts and images concerning the figure of Annah impose a set of beliefs and agendas on her, ones that support a very specific power dynamic between subject and artist – in which the former is assumed to be an unharmed muse, no matter what the truth may have been – and which have shaped extant narratives surrounding the real child or children who lived and inspired the painting. A 1950 *LIFE Magazine* issue described Annah, without evidence, as 'Gauguin's Faithless Javanese'; they are portrayed as a willing sexual partner of Gauguin's in film biopics of the artist, such as 1986's award-winning (and thoroughly vile in its depiction of the endangerment of children) *The Wolf at the Door*. Their image is used today in art history classes as an example of Gauguin's Primitivist oeuvre. Overwhelmingly, Annah has been depicted as supplementary, proof of Gauguin's closeness to the natives, a tantalising femme fatale, part of the myth of the genius artist, explorer and tamer of foreign wildnesses.

Paul Gauguin, *Annah La Javanaise, or Aita tamari vahine Judith te parari*
(The child-woman Judith is not yet breached), 1893–94

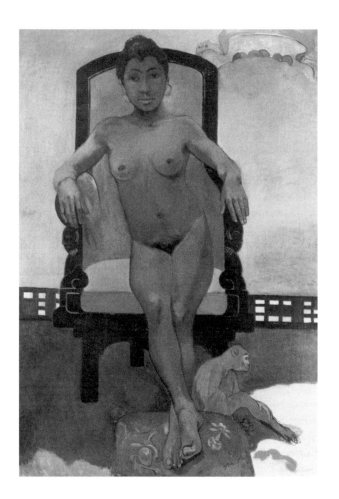

I'm convinced, however, that it's important to consider the notion, unexplored until now, that *Annah La Javanaise* is a portrait of a young girl in chronic pain. Why Annah in particular? Why pain? There is a perception that it is counterintuitive to describe people in paintings as potentially pained. But this is only because ocularcentric interpretations permeate the field of visual cultures. A depicted body is assumed to be unpained, until a certain set of cues that abled people understand as 'cues for pain' somehow prove that they are pained. Yet as those of us who live with chronic pain know, in photos and in the flesh there is often no way that another person can know we are in pain, nor to what degree. This has formed continual traumas in my own life, which I know that I am far from alone in experiencing.

Disabled[1] people are the largest minority in the world, and most of us live in or come from places that have borne the brunt of white supremacist political economies, in both the 'first world' and 'third world', whether lead-poisoned Flint, Michigan or environmentally threatened Kendeng, Indonesia, where opportunities for holistic healthcare have been starved by neoliberal economics and colonial legacies. The medical model of disability, which claims that all 'differences' must be 'healed' (in other words, stamped out), was so entrenched in Indonesian psyches by Dutch missionary hospital systems that I was only recently reminded of the fact that some Javanese deities are or have been disabled. These assumptions – abled until proven disabled – are deep-rooted, and intrinsically related to colonialist human classification systems. When we look at any image of any human, the default interpretation is that not only are they not in pain, but that the mere possibility of their painedness is preposterous. We have no understanding of bodies that exhibit no outer sign of pain according to abled norms, and yet are in pain. This makes Annah's pain a certain possibility.

Is this so far-fetched? That a child in the presence of an abusive older man, who seemed to revel in the intimation that they had a sexual relationship, would hurt? This does not mean she was only ever a victim. One story of Annah claims they robbed Gauguin of everything except his art. It's possible that Annah may have escaped. And even if they didn't, none of us are just victims of anything. We carry all of our lives in our bodies. These are stratified layers of emotion, complex memories kept in the sternum and soaked in the marrow. Annah would have had this kind of body too, a body that remembers, no matter how we choose to remember them.

I say that Annah could have been a pained body, a functioning pained body. Of course, the varieties of pain are infinite, from the aftermath of a stubbed toe, to fibromyalgia, to varying kinds of headaches. There are spectrums of pain's longevity, intensity, nature, origin, and crucially, spectrums of its meaning. Only Annah knows what was experienced by their body/ies. It is of urgent necessity to show the continuous, constant links between ableism, racism and sexism within colonial mechanisms. Bringing these to the fore illuminates how much we elide and deny histories of pain in human bodies, particularly

1. I take the word 'disabled' to mean a complex combination of socially imposed disabilities (the opposite of 'enabled') and other person-specific factors. It is my opinion that a person has the right to self-identify how they wish, as long as it does not hurt others; in line with my transnational community of disability justice activists, I prefer 'disabled person' to 'person with a disability', the latter term often contributing to further stigma of 'otherness' or 'difference' – and eugenicist urges to eradicate it.

vulnerable human bodies, such as those of Annah. Portrayed as vivacious and lively, their wellbeing was profoundly at risk.

So here we go. Let's consider and imagine Annah differently, many different Annahs, Annah as infinite possibilities. The truth is the same distance from our grasp as the 1890s; truth kept with, and belonging to, only them and all the many possible thems.

*

Annah La Javanaise is a painting created in France, which affixes a name to its subject belonging to those who come from a densely populated Southeast Asian island. The painting uses bright colours, and is meant to be placed upright, meaning, vertically as the subject is presented. When the piece is listed – in galleries, museums, libraries, and within the electric flow of her image – his name comes first. His name, then Annah's, then Judith's:

Paul Gauguin, *Annah the Javanese, or Aita tamari vahine Judith te parari* (*The child-woman Judith is not yet breached*), 1893-94. Oil on canvas, 45 1/4 × 31 1/2 in. (116 × 81 cm.) Private Collection.

This is a rectangle-shaped piece of commerce. A person is sitting on a chair, taking up the frame's space. We infer: this is Annah the Javanese. There is an unnamed creature alongside Annah, but it is not Judith: it is a monkey at their feet. Annah is smiling like Mona Lisa, but they are naked. The background wall is peach-terracotta.

What on earth is Judith doing in that title? you might ask. You might well ask. Judith Molard posed as a full-frontal nude model for Gauguin in sessions that were put to a stop by her mother, Ida, once they were discovered. *Annah La Javanaise* could have been, in fact, an amalgamated body of this girl and another. But it is, in the end, Annah whom it is safer and easier for Gauguin to objectify, to twist into an image of sexual openness. And it is emphasised that the child-girl Judith has not been breached – with the implication that this is not the case for Annah.

Annah has the body of a presumed cis-girl. 'Child-Woman'. They have pubic hair, possible snail trail, round breasts. Probably a B-cup, perhaps a C when, if, they get their period. Their hair is tied up. Their earrings are looped and golden. Their legs are crossed at the ankles, on a green cushion. They are naked and palatial.

Annah was around thirteen, they say, so perhaps, if in a menstruating body, they had not yet had their first period. Or perhaps they had, though the figure on the chair shows no signs of bleeding.

What is this Private Collection? The terms of possession keep Annah La Javanaise's current owners to themselves.

*

Annah sits on blue upholstery in a carved wooden chair.

Would you feel comfortable being naked with a monkey at your feet? Would you be afraid of it biting you? Who would you allow to see you sitting in a chair with your legs crossed at your ankles, with nothing on but earrings and perhaps a hair clip?

*

In historical documents, Annah is given biographical attributes that are completely disparate from one to the next – 'half-Malay, half-Indian';

'half-Indonesian, half-Dutch'; 'mulatto'; 'Polynesian', as a Tate Library archive entry has it. Originally, she was labelled as 'Javanese', but the varied writing on her origins allows for slippages in the interstices of these biographical facts. It doesn't matter what colony this person is from, these clashing documents suggest, as long as they are from a colony.

Over the past eight years, I have seen photos of brown, girl-presenting children, with faces that could have been from entirely different people, all labelled as Annah. I have seen two photos of exactly the same brown, girl-presenting body, labelled both 'Hannah la Javanaise, Paul Gauguin's mistress' and 'Tohotaua of Polynesia who posed for Paul Gauguin'. They have never been able to tell us apart. When it comes to the object of colonisation, the details aren't important. All that matters is that details, people, are possessed and possessable.

That their origins are written as varied and clashing gives rise to this understanding: Annah could have been many kinds of bodies. They could have been trans. They could have hated the pronoun 'they' and preferred 'she', and in this case as in others, she could have been autistic or otherwise neurodivergent, could have been D/deaf, could have limped. She or they or him or dia (the Indonesian gender-neutral pronoun for all) could have been in a non-normative body, and chosen not to disclose this. Perhaps non-disclosure would have been a small window to less vulnerability, a little more safety in the terrifying world these child-figure(s) were already in.

*

'maybe the body is the only question an answer can't extinguish'
Ocean Vuong, *Night Sky with Exit Wounds*

*

From *Paul Gauguin: An Erotic Life* by Nancy Mowll Mathews

'Alternatively seductive and bullying in his manner... Although he did not hesitate to physically abuse both men and women and evidently was titillated by their submission, he also imagined the pleasurable sensation of receiving such abuse. His many paintings of Eve frightened by the snake attest to his belief in the eroticism of both rape and submission.'

*

An object sits on a chair in this painting, in the shape of a woman made of brown oil. Primate at her feet, whole nudity stretched out. Hair in a bun, bum perched on seat's edge.

Is this a 'nature painting'? Is this natural? *Annah La Javanaise. Aita tamari vahina Judith te parari.* With its title in French and Tahitian, the work has at least four cultural components that can be discerned: (1) French, (2) a reference to the Javanese, a culture on the island of Java, Indonesia's most populated island, and therefore (3) Indonesian, the country now fourth most populated in the world, that emerged as independent in 1945, its borders including Java, the island on which Indonesia's capital Jakarta resides, and (4) Tahitian, a language invoked by Gauguin to suggest to others that he was close to 'savages', to the exotic, to primitive peoples whose art he aped, whose young girls he captured for future private art collections.

Khairani Barokka, *Annah #733.2: Floor Projection for 'Annah: Nomenclature' at the ICA*, 2018. Digital illustration for performance installation.

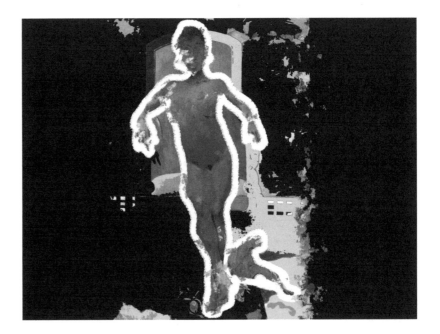

Despite the flattening of her identity, there remains the possibility that Annah's body had pulsating parts which were nerve-sensitised, vulnerable to variable jolts, waves and oceans of pain. As many kinds of pain as water, Frenchwaters, Tahitianwaters, Javanesewaters, Indonesianwaters, Englishwaters, traversing, concurrently – pain could have been a hazy drizzle in the arm, a shudder of rain, a deluge of sea; it could have been of different intensities, ebbing in some collections of cells, flowing in others.

Once a professor I know said of the painting something to the effect of, 'Yes, she could be disabled and in pain, she is tilted.' But those of us who know pain know: we can assume Olympian positions of strength and endurance, years at a time, holding it puckered in ligaments, giving no sign of our painedness to abled folk. We can smile widely, with no one but ourselves the wiser. Our bodies could be imploding internally and, perhaps because we have been disbelieved so routinely, we may not even signal in an ablenormative way that we are in distress. In addition, when a body is experiencing acute pain, it may be to such a degree that the human brain is overwhelmed, bewildered, and causes behaviour inscrutable to others. Sometimes we must appear abled for employment purposes, such as when sitting as an artist's model, for a man whose child later wrote about how his father had hit his mother. Though Gauguin's son wrote of his father's domestic abuse, and Gauguin's over-familiar relationships with a plethora of children are documented in numerous archival sources, not a single authority figure stepped in to apprehend him for any suspected crime. Crimes, after all, are relative according to societal framings of them, their time and place, and the protection that was thought deserved by people such as Marie Jade, Judith Molard, Jeanne Schuffenecker, Teha'amana, Pahura a Tai, and Annah.

Annah's situation made her more vulnerable to chronic pain, and she was vulnerable due to many factors: a young, brown, femme-presenting child in Paris of uncertain citizenship with no documented guardians, with a history of child labour according to accounts that she began Parisian life as a domestic worker or sex worker; very likely an ongoing survivor of abuse at the hands of an older, colonial white man who was surrounded primarily by other older, white men who condoned if not contributed to and perpetuated this abuse; set up as a sexual rival to the girls her age she was in contact with; profoundly isolated with a lack of holistic healthcare and wellbeing. All of these elements meant she was at risk of injury from trauma, which can result in chronic pain.

What if these were the painting's titles?

Portrait of a Child in Pain.
Portrait of a Nude Child in Pain.
Portrait of Nude Child Annah in Pain (The Child Judith Has Not Been Breached).

Gauguin's fantasies of young girls could actually have been fantasies of young girls in severe pain. Entertain this notion. Stay with it. It is a clear option.

What is this 'nature' Gauguin thought he was spelling out, if an abled painter is unaware of the nuances of the sittee's internal states? I assume the painter is abled and not in pain. Do I assume that the painted body is not in pain? Why, and why not? Do I assume Gauguin was not in pain, the tortured artist? After all, the mystique surrounding Gauguin has not only been that he was closer to 'savage' native cultures in his wildness, which led to his travels and associations with brown subjects, but that he suffered for his eccentricity, his alienation from valorised bourgeois French values. In that article 'Gauguin's Faithless Javanese', Annah is blamed for Gauguin's financial woes in the lead-up to his death – perversely, she is painless, he is pained by her. Stories of white male artists, who are the 'great', the 'geniuses', in Eurocentric art history curricula, are littered with justifications for their harmful behaviour. The actual power dynamics between them and their muses are magically reversed. As I consider the power dynamics here, I de-intensify Paul Gauguin's pain in light of how vulnerable he made Annah.

I think of Annah as oil on canvas in an unnamed private collection (a source I shall keep anonymous has told me of a diabolically wealthy family which she thinks is in possession of the painting), and also as a series of pixels. Ones and zeroes, JPEGs, GIFs, PNGs, screenshots, Google Image searches, on endless screens. Alive in the cloud. The message here is repeated, subtle cues we receive every day in an ablenormative world about visual images: 'She is abled. She is not in pain.' Yet the notion that a body is either 'in pain' or 'not in pain', one or the other, rather than, for instance, 'I'm fine, though now that I have a minute to rest, I realise my muscles feel exhausted' or 'I've lived with chronic pain that fluctuates from acute severity to bearability, depending on a bunch of factors. Right now I'd say it's five out of ten in my chest and two out of ten in my arm, if you want to use a flawed numerical system.' Abled assumptions of a monolithic, binary system for painedness are treacherous, and often deceitful.

A person can pose for a portrait sitting and be pained. A person can feel it acutely the longer they sit, or perceive it as a dull ache. Or forget about the pain, because it's lasted so long in the body that the mind has constructed a defence of many neurons that allows them to live so pained, in varying degrees.

The images here pose the question: where are the traces of possible pain in all forms of Annah La Javanaise as image: .JPEG, .PNG, screenshot, Google Search? I believe they have always been there.

The FAQs website for the Register for Artist Models (RAM), the UK's professional association for artist models and tutors, says:

'(3) Have you the patience and stamina required to keep very still for up to 45 minutes at a time, regardless of whatever discomfort (sometimes pain) you may be in? Sometimes you will be required to return to the same awful pose after a short break. Indeed, the same pose may last for several weeks. In time you learn what to avoid, to some extent, and you also become a bit tougher, but you will never avoid pain and discomfort entirely in this job.'

Here it is prudent to remind ourselves that Annah, of course, is never recorded as having been paid monetarily for her services as a muse.

Over the past eight years, I've created many multiform Annah scenarios, numbered randomly to emphasise the infinite nature of their possibilities, which includes, finally, the possibility that there are worlds in which the child is somehow safe.

*

Annah #8,925 Conveys A Message To You

Schoolgirls learn about me in classrooms. They cup my breasts like a mug of hot tea, leaves picked from blurry lands, inconsequential plantations.

What is the term for this: erasure? Diminishment? Of humming we still feel in our bodies, and would rather forget, or better yet, transform into a substance of gentleness, protective momentum, beyond healed scar, beyond the right not to forgive.

I feel a constant panic, the panic of not being understood by yet another, and another, and another. They wear tartan skirts and red backpacks; I only notice the ones my age. That schoolgirls are taught about my image as benign is in no way benign. It is caught up in all the ways we revere male 'geniuses' so long after their deaths, so long after the deaths of us as muses, as more than muses. Our humanity is boiling hot to the blood as a cauldron, overspilling again and again within the confines of our skin; this is not taught to the schoolgirls. There is a constant mad rush to be known, and to be home. My inside stirrings have been denied not repeatedly but interminably, without end, and so it is their reality that reigns, that imperils me, that sickens me from within. And my hands begin to hurt.

Every time you try to thrash through the wall beyond which, you hope, you will find peace and a whole sense of selfhood that thrives, you are shaken by it, the wall thrashes back, thunders against your shoulders as it throws you upon itself.

The monkey-fed room you have been thrust into is on fire. Walls of this room become limits of skin.

Something has been damaged to wrecking point.

It began before it began. When I saw him and soon after, his paintings. I realised what he did in Tahiti, to those girls, and how he would make the painting with my name as its title. How my body would be on a plane, oiled, a representation foretold, as it had been for other women whose language I did not speak, whose customs I did not understand. I understood that, like a very small child, a Parisian not-brown would look at our skins, as though deciphering the remnants of a hunt, and draw circles around us.

And earlier, when I set foot in France for the first time, and the weight of universal unsafety descended on my black-haired head with every look that came my way, that wanted me gone or captured, a monkey in Europe, a curiosity. It began when I knew I would leave Java, and when my mother died it began very quietly there, with her last breath. As wicked as living often is, I want my mother in it. As wicked as living is, I want the strange thing that is life.

*

Annah #67

So I wake up in monochrome, and someone is asking 'Why would you think of her in chronic pain?' And then it's more than a person asking, it's many. I scratch at the surface of the canvas from within, and find I can't breathe. To realise respiration was never an option when your flesh is paint, what a godawful relief. So I throw my head back and laugh, because I realise I am inanimate, I am a figurine on a canvas, there's no air to go in my lungs. How am I even sure there are lungs in here when I can't even remember the monkey's name; can I be sure of what I learned of anatomy? I try to remember the place where I could have learned of two bags of hollow lung splayed in a chest, symmetrical, heaving in and out again.

Back in the village there was a school. Did I go? The Dutch weren't allowed to teach us, learning came from the mosque and aunties – Bu Des – around us. Rattan was used as a ruler might be in the white schools, rapped against walls and floors for attention. There is a lesson I knew before I knew it, which is that the maps of a woman's anatomy we know came about through torture of women whose skins were brown – slaves used for medical experiments, that led to OB/GYN discoveries. The sexual reproductive system was delineated this way. I don't remember the year I am in. I've banged my head, it seems, or were these voices always rushing, retching towards my body.

'Why would you think of her in chronic pain?
in chronic pain?
in chronic pain?'

And I think of when P. nearly choked on a fishbone and then chucked a decanter at my neck, screaming that came from the wine in his veins about how he'd hit his wife whenever he could, so I'd better get the fuck on my knees and suck him for cooking this shit.

I somehow also know that his son will write about remembering this, father bloodying his mother.

In museums, there are so many girls who might be mistaken for me. I have been mistaken for them. I run my hands across their hair, all the world greyscale, in a different colour register from his. I lift up their hair with their permission, see scabs healing over on the napes from his hands. One of the girls tells me it is the Christian year 2020. The Javanese calendar: Jumadiawal – 1953 Wawu, Sengara Langkir.

'Don't worry', I tell all of them, 'I have a plan,' and we leave stretched out canvases together for a secret pot of retribution.

*

Annah #45 on the Water

I went to sit far by the river, as the river is also the ocean.
As marine goddess Nyi Roro Kidul came and
took me in her arms as a cauldron of fear, in a dream,
telling of such things that I now know. And currently
he is napping, so I may open into the sun. Napping as
a prerequisite for busy waves in miniature and fervent,
against my ankles. They call this liquid the Seine, and
I say it is the Java Sea. Oil rises thick to the top,
against banks; I swim deep.

SARAH FLETCHER

COUNTRY MATTERS

DEDICATION

Flamingo, urchin, bestiaric beast:
Paroling city matters, you re-form
From pigeon's dirty feather to a quill.

A parlour game: we reach the dovetailing
Between those singing spasmic pities that
We summon, and the dank urbanity

You wreak. It comes to punish this reserve.
Love: whether zoo, circus, menagerie,
All matters of a name more so than form,

Let us rush towards autowilderness,
Strifed with wet, chaostic humours. 1
Erotic prescience : I sense us : one.

We've taken flyte, so let us rest in shelter,
Into the original of the world,
Nothing can stop our loved country from mattering.

ONE

*

There is a woman turning a woman turning
itself on

Sick hydra starting up   I dream
of sea becoming seaworthy to sea

The sea drownsy   in its offensive capability

Drownsy Baby   thirsting in its sleep   *Hush now*

Totemic fetish or mnemonic logo :   her offensive cheep :   untid'ly starting
up for the tide :   *cheap*

*

You cannot scry in your own silver when
its ripples split the vision

They cannot peer into a depth they've mined   and filled

Selfsang in their own gags   Dull drams overfilled

                                        —spilling unward

Eat your eyesight, bastard   *Ring yourself unfit*

*

Q: Where has this water gone? Why disappear?

A: Add an arch to the middle of valour. There's your answer.

In the mean time, build a city   Then build a countryside
for balance

Now, not sea at all   They become

ardor's coldened shoulder   Ardor eccentric
Radiating inward

Throttling at different purposes and speeds.

*

TWO

An altared state urned in a loss of verse
Severed then served with coming of the morning
My love has earned this insurrective swerve
That seeks to crash the calming of his mourning

*

You rest inequality

If I was embedded in a painscape, it'd be different

Q: Where do you rest?
A: Camped out
in the bedazzled house
of his runtish fantasy

His House Believes ...

As it is now, there is
an asterisk to every kiss

Let me rest
in that nest of those pink, electric branches

There, there is safety

*

THREE

To have a handle on something is to have the capacity to turn
it on or off

*

What I cuse him of I cuse myself

*

When they are together, their shape
is endless and content

The sea drinking the sea   The sea is drinking
                                                              the sea

*

The vulvic octopus dies with her young
Meanwhile, I: waste   with my   youth

The staggering dear does not accept my hand,
fawning and shrill. Cast off from my ilk, my hart.

*

FOUR

Dysgenic bodie's calling back to you,
Consumed and mated. Her dysphoric flesh;
Locked within your own twin study; She'll
do anything, at last, to prove your bad.

Gravity holds each wave in vassalage.
Without gods, there is none mastered;
O gypsum child: I see through your age,
Such wind wrinkles water alabastered.

*

Fair Access more than anything
                          : I wish them will

THE GARDEN OF LOVE'S SLEEP
After Messiaen's Turangalîla

Dinner is poured   Then: his hand on mine –

Instead
of sensation
I receive

The dream
Of two green peacocks
Pouring smooth grails of touch
Each across the other

Necks arched in extravagant,
Romantic love.

*

Insomnia swells a congealing city
Congests each head with   phrases:

'A horse called Horus or just Birdy'   'A wine press named War on Earth':

Those haute contour contraptions from the ancién French regime

*

Áwake   Who is with me?   Whó
Will unhook
The colours' ruffles from sunrise
Each by each?

When we talk about Manifestos
I feel white
Doves sprung from a Magician's
Sleeves on sleeves
Release

In this state
And at this event

*

On open caboose   On train to Vladivostok

Mosquitoes are breeding quickly in the dark

Clouds' petticoats uncross   Cross again
Flashing the sun from which we cannot hide
Which catches us
Spoiled and sticky

Like Love's Sunday

*

The emperor's clothes are very beautiful   and they
Are very real   I remember them like the song
That climbs back to me in snatches: *Harbouring*
The antiseptic beauty   `   *Harpooning*
the August moon   *Haranguing*
the something   something   something   Noon

*

Have we slept? I've found us
Flabberghastly   Clean and glamorose
Like the courtesan   who appears here
And all other places   in a new state
age   dress   civility
Having forgot the crashing sound of a beating door
The stench of the night closing in
Endarkening   O Carrion!

*

At last

Something beautiful arrives!

The equal weightéd phrase
That leaves your mouth and the sky
At the same time

SAIDIYA HARTMAN   INTERVIEW

The first time I encountered Saidiya Hartman, she was a voice in *salt.*, an award-winning play by artist and performer Selina Thompson. Woven carefully into the play's text, Hartman's words guide Thompson as she embarks on a cargo ship voyage, with the intention of re-charting the path of the trans-Atlantic slave trade. The effect is seamless. Over the course of the production, Thompson offers excerpts from Hartman's 2007 book *Lose Your Mother: A Journey Along the Atlantic Slave Route*, in which Hartman shares her own account of tracing the same history, in Ghana, years earlier.

Born and raised in New York City, a place she still calls home, Hartman is a professor at Columbia University within the department of English. Across each of her books, *Scenes of Subjection: Terror, Slavery and Self-Making in Nineteenth-Century America* (1997), *Lose Your Mother* and *Wayward Lives, Beautiful Experiments: Intimate Histories of Social Upheaval* (2019), Hartman's writing unpacks what she terms 'the afterlife of slavery'. With an emphasis on the word *life*, Hartman is relentless in fleshing out the ongoing intricacies with which the trade formed – and persists in forming – the racialised relations of our present world.

Her mastery, however, is in how she does this, how her encounters with archival material – inventories documenting the enslaved, photographs, songs, names, or the sheer lack of them – become stimuli for a narrative technique that stories the silence of loss without speaking over it. In her 2008 essay, 'Venus in Two Acts', she calls this methodology 'critical fabulation': an 'impossible writing that attempts to say that which resists being said'; an account of history written both 'with and against the archive', often bending time, rendering the past, present and future coterminous. As Chicago-based poet and vocalist Jamila Woods sings, *Look what they did to my sisters, last century, last week*. Over the last two decades, Hartman has made it her life's work to gaze incredibly closely. Never with the clinical detachment of an outsider. Always, as she writes, from 'within the circle' of black diasporic culture and thought.

Where *Scenes of Subjection* and *Lose Your Mother* deal more intimately with the workings of enslavement, *Wayward Lives*, her most recent book, attends to the vibrant urban lives of black women born after emancipation. Reading as a long meditation, *Wayward Lives* cel-ebrates a generation of forgotten women who chose to live freely within the cages of their cities; to love multiply, beyond the state's oppressive dictates of gender, race and class.

I met Hartman recently when she was in London to give a talk at Birkbeck. Sitting across the table from her, as we worked our way through lunchtime sushi, Hartman had the aura of someone for whom introspection comes naturally. She is as measured and deliberate in person as she is on the page. I believe, too, that her respect for silence – by which I mean: the private doorway to deep thought that only silence can provide – is what enables her to write so fluidly into the voids and failures of history. In an age where action or thought is so often paired with a broadcast on social media, Hartman's quietude is a needful reminder that only the work truly counts. VICTORIA ADUKWEI BULLEY

THE WHITE REVIEW   Looking back to when you first started out on your journey as an academic, as someone interested in storytelling, in archives, did you have a clear vision of what you wanted to achieve back then?

SAIDIYA HARTMAN   I think one thing that I accepted from early on was the sense that I was a wailer. Partly in the Bob Marley and the Wailers sense of what it means to offer witness, to recognise yourself as involved in the project of remembering what the world has chosen to forget and to write about black people with the rigour and depth commensurate with our experience. It is a very feminised labour of trying to express and to hold this collective affect of black folks; to witness and not to pretend that things aren't bad, that we aren't in this seemingly interminable struggle and that we have not been living this dispossession so long.

I had that desire when I wrote my first poem as a middle-schooler. I wanted to be a witness.

TWR   One of the things I think about a lot is the question of how we care for ourselves whilst doing archival work. We are not merely engaging with information, but human lives, and attempting to respectfully bring these lives into the light. I wonder about the effects that this has on us as black artists, writers and thinkers. How have you navigated this in your work?

SH   I agree with you that it is really difficult work, and it does take a toll psychically. I remember what may have been my first or second reading of *Lose Your Mother*, and I was reading with a South African novelist, Yvette Christiansë, who had written a novel about slavery and infanticide. I was reading from 'So Many Dungeons' – that chapter in the book about being in the dungeon of the slave castle – and suddenly I just lost it. I found myself in tears publicly, and I hadn't anticipated that. It was as if there was this huge, huge wave of grief that I was carrying and that I was obviously processing in the writing, but clearly *hadn't* processed. There was that residue. After the reading, these three older black women – I think of them as the three old crones – came up to me, and they said *you can leave the hold now*. If you're really present, then what is undeniable is the devastation and loss and geno-cide. All the death and destruction for the purposes of capital accumulation - trade - still structures our lives. We are living in the world created by the transatlantic slave trade.

I began *Wayward Lives*, a book about freedom and beauty, with the simple feeling that *I can't write another book about slavery*. I couldn't bear another decade in the archive of slavery. I do actually have another small set of essays that are about slavery, but I just needed to put them down.

TWR   It's conflicting because there's no wish to be wounded – more so than we already are – by these realities, but the scale of what we're looking at is so heavy that it wouldn't be right not to be changed by it.

SH   Especially because the world largely has denied the violence that was absolutely necessary for the trade to unfold and develop. Black thinkers and writers have been absolutely central to trans-forming our understanding of the Atlantic slave trade by acknowledging the scope and depth of its violence, its terror. It's been absolutely necessary work.

TWR   *Lose Your Mother* maps your experience of being in Ghana – a location significantly affect-ed by the transatlantic slave trade – and searching for traces left by those who were captured and transported to the Americas. How did you come to write it?

SH   In a way it was a strange thing that I even wrote *Lose Your Mother*. I do say, explicitly, that it wasn't a 'back-to-my-roots' journey, but nonethe-less I was on the trail of the dispossessed: those who had been made captives and exchanged in the trade. The character of the archive in Ghana at the time was not textual but one of landscape, it was an archive of the unsaid – and I really didn't know how to work with that. I was on a Fulbright fellowship and I thought *Oh my God, I don't have a book to write after all this*. Kofi Anyidoho, a professor at the University of Ghana, encouraged me to fold my own personal experience into the encounter, which was really the last thing I wanted to do because I'm a very private person. But I think that what he saw, that I didn't – at the time – was how deep the resonance of emotion was around this his-tory, and how deeply marked diasporic subjects are by it. Even beyond our own awareness, you know? So I thought, OK, *can I actually do this*? And then it just became necessary to write the book.

TWR   You were there in the late nineties?
SH   I was there in 1997-98. That was a radically different world. I feel that as a result of those

diasporic encounters there is a very different discourse on the ground today.

TWR   I was 7 in 1998, so I can't speak to that moment, but as a Ghanaian in the diaspora today it does seem to have become important to make that connection to the African continent. It feels very much in vogue.

SH   Now it's very much in vogue, and today there are so many individuals, from the US and the Caribbean, travelling to Ghana with questions about slavery and who are engaged in a dialogue and exchange with Ghanaians. But back then I was surprised by how seemingly out of sort my questions were to Ghanaians. The questions that I was raising about those who were lost into the trade were met with resistance, or hostility, or indifference, or unknowing. And yet African novelists had been dealing with these things *forever*–

TWR   Forever!

SH   So that was just so interesting. It was like, wait – but this is the home of Ayi Kwei Armah and Ama Ata Aidoo. There was Yambo Ologuem and Ben Okri, you know? All these African novelists. *Lose Your Mother* is about disenchanting a certain myth of belonging, of roots, to actually try to find another language of connection. I think there are people who never get to the last chapter, 'Fugitive Dreams', so they never understand that.

TWR   And you *have* to get there–

SH   You have to get there! Because it does happen, but it's a journey. I realised that people weren't getting there. I was doing readings and I'd read the last chapter and so many people said they had no memory of that last chapter. I think they thought that I gave up. I also think that they didn't understand the impact of African writers on my work, even though I titled one of the chapters 'The Famished Road' – that's a clear homage. I include traces of Ayi Kwei Armah, Achille Mbembe... so there's the presence of that influence.

TWR   I can only imagine what a strange feeling it must have been to notice that among your readers. It's almost as though they haven't read the book that you wrote.

SH   At a certain moment – and this is very recently – people got to the end of the book; I think they did so as a result of the readings I was doing. Also people began to read it in relation to

NourbeSe Philip's *Zong* and Dionne Brand's *Map to the Door of No Return*. Only then did people start to mention this other language of relation that I was writing about – one that's not about origins but about reversals of history and the aspirations and struggles that we share. The political scientist James Scott has done all this work on the anarchist traditions of South Asian peasants, and I would say there's also a history of radical struggle that has its origins on the African continent. One of the things I wanted to ask was, 'What are the histories of struggle against these predatory state formations, and do they shape and inform a diasporic imagination?' That too, is part of the language of Black Radicalism. It's about our fugitive dreams.

TWR   Which is to say that the site of union is not so much the wound but the dream. Maintaining that awareness of our variously common and distinct struggles or origins as black people, whilst focusing on the question: *What is the dream, and where are we going?*

SH   Exactly.

TWR   How would you describe your process?

SH   I research and write in separate stages. I read widely and takes tons and tons of notes, and then I begin writing. I rarely consult the notes, but simply begin writing. What I recall most clearly – or the details that emerge from the file or document – are the beginnings of the story or narrative. What I remember and where I start is with the detail that is the equivalent of the punctum, the moment of a life, the shape of an object, the darkness of a room, that solicits me, most often because it represents an opening or a detour.

TWR   Your work serves as a guide for writing into the empty spaces of archives and memory, particularly your methodology of 'critical fabulation' – a way of imagining one's route through voids. I am also thinking of Christina Sharpe's recent writing around 'wake work' – her framing this work as an expression of *care* – which is also such a brilliant term for these explorations.

SH   One of the things that I really love about Christina's book [*In the Wake: On Blackness and Being*] which I don't think would have been possible, a decade ago, is its engagement with the Atlantic in relation to the Mediterranean and its capacious account of the black experience across Europe, Africa and the Americas. I'm sure you feel this personally – you're black in a way that your Ghanaian parents never were. What does blackness mean for the experience of African migrants and their brutal racialisation, and also what does it mean for first, second and third generation black Europeans to be considered outsiders within their national contexts? It's so much about time and place. Thinking blackness in these terms had no resonance whatsoever in Ghana when I was there. Sharpe is able to expand our thinking in this comparative and nuanced way because the language of blackness has become shared and universalised.

TWR   Here in the UK, our histories of black radicalism have faced a lot of erasure – perhaps one reason why we're still searching for ways to articulate the specificities of our being here.
SH   Part of my own black experience is a consequence of growing up in New York City. Many of the friends I went to school with were black but we didn't speak the same languages at home. They were from Haiti, Panama, from the Dutch-speaking Caribbean, so that blackness was already so differentiated. Blackness was never really defined by sameness. Because of my father's family's history of migration there were some people in the family who were *never* black – and there you also see the work of identification, or *dis*identification. Blackness doesn't presume any unanimity of culture, or reference, you know? Even as the structural condition is shared. People who were outsiders, not from New York – it could be a white person or a black person who came from the South or the Midwest, a much more homogeneous cultural formation – would say, how can you look at someone and tell if they're Panamanian or Haitian? I took difference for granted. I had a friend who was a southerner who moved to New York, and her landlord was Jamaican and his wife was from Grenada, and she thought that to have a Caribbean identity was to say that you were not black, because she'd grown up in a context where people were only black or white. She was a fair-skinned black woman, and still the lines were solid.

TWR   Let's talk about the figure of the circle because it appears in all of your books. It arises when you speak about writing 'from inside the circle', it comes up when instances of dance occur in your texts, and it seems to me that there's something very black about it as signifier. What are your thoughts on the circle as a symbol, as a framework,

and as a mode of relation within blackness?
SH   You're right in that there are these three spaces or architectures that are absolutely foundational to my work: the Atlantic, the hold, and the circle. And I think that the circle is a central figure when trying to describe black radical imaginaries and anti-slavery philosophy, from Frederick Douglass's description of the circle as a space of sociality and radical thought, to the historian Sterling Stuckey, who looks at circle formations in African American culture, tracing them to Congo culture – specifically, the Bakongo cosmogram. So all that is to say that I think you're right that the circle is this deep, diasporic formation that travels with us. It's so rich with the potential of relation, possibility, care, other modes of understanding – it's the knowledge we have and make with one another. And that's why Douglass is so pivotal for me. It may seem like nonsense to the outside world, but *in here* we know it is a tome of philosophy. It resonates with Édouard Glissant's discussion about 'the right to opacity'. *Lose Your Mother* closes with a circle formation. In Gwolu, these young girls give me the possibility of another language of relation – and I think that I became aware of the gift *after* the fact; it wasn't that I was trying to build or even assume a connection. In *Wayward Lives* there is a beautiful stark image of the Atlantic, and as I was writing, I reflected on why it was important to have this image in the book. It is one of the spaces or milieux that define blackness. Alongside the circle, the hold, the colony, the native quarter, the carceral landscape. The circle forms inside the enclosure and even in the worst circumstances, there is making and relation.

TWR   What was the genesis story of *Wayward Lives, Beautiful Experiments*?
SH   When I started writing the book, I had no idea of its scale and ambition. The book began with my encounter with the girl in the Thomas Eakins photograph and trying to account for her life. What was the life of a young black girl like a few decades after the legal abolition of slavery and in anticipation of the new century? The photograph was a condensation of centuries of black existence, an enduring image of captivity and commodification, and an image that raised questions about the meaning of freedom. It was an image of temporal entanglement.

TWR   Can we talk about the word *wayward*?

I love this word because there's something in it that suggests going rogue, going off-course, but also finding a course; searching for one. Not just moving outside of imposed limits, but being in favour of making a new way. It seems to me to be the key word, the keystone in *Wayward Lives, Beautiful Experiments*. How did you arrive at it?

SH   Wayward was so resonant with other terms – detour, errant, fugitive – and it is a word that brings to mind this practice of variance or deviation, so it seemed richly suggestive. In the chapter 'Wayward: A Short Entry on the Possible', it's connected to all of these other words like *anarchy* and *queer* and *unruly*, but there was something about the gendered character of it that was exactly right, it seemed both old-fashioned and absolutely contemporary. The wayward girl is the girl who won't succumb to or obey the gender script. The challenge when describing black women's lives, black women's radical practices, is that they're always subsumed or asterisked to a larger category. I just needed to say no, their practice *is* the category, you know? And this notion of being a footnote to everything else is what waywardness enabled me to challenge, it seemed an organic term for describing the radical and disobedient imaginary of young black women – so that's why I liked it. How do we understand black radical imaginaries without understanding how central girls and women are to those projects?

I remember once giving a talk and people were nodding their heads like *yes, yes, yes, but why not just call that queer?* It's because queer is already loaded and known; queer has also been a category that in some respects has effaced the intellectual labour and practice of black women. Few think queer as in Nella Larsen. So *wayward* seemed more richly suggestive, and then all of those other terms were folded in as a part of its definition.

TWR   It also seems to me that there's an order here – a sense that queerness comes *under* the heading of waywardness, not vice versa.

SH   That's exactly right, queerness is one articulation of a wayward project, but there's something about the general waywardness that is blackness that I wanted to underscore. And *then* there's the queer, the anarchic – all of those are attributes of waywardness. I think your question might have been better than my answer...!

TWR   Whilst reading *Wayward Lives*, a poem that came to mind often was Lucille Clifton's

'why some people be mad at me sometimes'. She writes, 'they ask me to remember / but they want me to remember / their memories / and i keep on remembering / mine.' At the heart of that poem is an expression of both refusal and repetition, which resonates deeply with your book.

SH   I think that refusal is the everyday practice of saying no to those structures that consign us to death and to subordination, and that refusal happens on multiple scales. So one of the young women in the book, Esther Brown, is described as being *not afraid to smash things up* and that way of being is a response to a world that is trying to consign her to a place that's less-than, and so she says *Esther Brown won't take that*. It's an assertion of her refusal to servitude, to subordination, and to the kind of valuelessness produced by anti-black-ness. That's one aspect of refusal, and I think that repetition – or maybe I might say, the *refrain*, those circulating refrains – just echo and echo across time and space and we can think of the refrain as echoing from Harriet Jacobs inside her loophole of retreat, to Assata Shakur, or to #SayHerName. There are these utterances that are recurring and they continue to animate struggle, they continue to remind us of the possible. Lucille Clifton's work is such a resource of these refrains: why I, everyday, celebrate the act of survival, why I celebrate that *something has tried to kill me and failed* – surviving in a world where I'm *not meant to survive*. The refrains of Harriet Jacobs or Tubman or Sojourner Truth or Bessie Head resound in my words and determine how we think about our condition, and the pasts that reside in our now—

TWR   As though we are inhabiting our own sense of time, wherein everything exists at once—

SH   Everything all at once! And the way in which we are still trying to make good the proclamations of over a century ago; the struggle to be treated as if human flesh. Those patterns or statements or refrains - this collective utterance - also provide an architecture or a grounding for *Wayward Lives*. This collective resource of black women's thought that is Toni Morrison *and* Angela Davis *and* Maryse Condé and all the black women thinkers and writers whose words are tools for survival.

TWR   In the text you use italicisation rather than footnotes, and as I read I realised how truly essential this is. It imbues the text with an orality that traditional citation doesn't achieve.

SH   It was exactly my intention for the text to be polyphonic, to conjure the multivocality of the chorus and the spoken character of utterance. One of the things that was really important for me to convey was the sensorium of black urban space, and that is so much about sound, right? The intimacy and proximity and overhearing of this shared utterance. I wanted to create that sense of not just a spoken text but a text that's created by this multiplicity of utterance and that sometimes it speaks in multiple ways, like *girl, you're too much*, you know? The description of the 'too much' of blackness or the 'too much' of the wayward and not wanting to be disciplined by the disciplinary apparatus. In large measure, what the practice of citation does is reproduce intellectual hierarchies. Whose words must be accounted for? Whose words are endowed with autonomy or must be treated as if valuable and private property, as opposed to the kind of taken-for-granted utterances that are credited to no one in particular? I wanted to level all of that.

TWR   And that takes a beautiful leap of faith because not every reader will recognise every reference in italics, but there's a chance that at some point they will. It reminds me of the use of sampling in hip-hop.
SH   You're totally, absolutely right about that. And certainly, in the music, we understand that – there's a great range of reference or resonance or sampling that comprises the work, yet you can enjoy the piece of music whether or not you know the allusions and references, but when you can hear all of it, you're like *oh my God!* VèVè Clark had this lovely phrase called 'diaspora literacy', and she used this to describe Condé's novel *Hérémakhonon* because that novel has such a wide range of diasporic reference. Condé takes for granted that sense of *OK, you need to get on board – there's a black world that is being described here* and refuses to explain or instruct. So I think that's a way of centring the *within the circle* formation in that it's not about leading an unknowing reader carefully into this world, rather it's like oh, you know what, there's a vast range of reference and ideas in play and you're welcome to come in – but the more you know, the more you hear.

TWR   There's a striking line in *Wayward Lives* that reads 'everything from the first ship to the woman found hanging in her cell'. This made me think of Sarah Reed's death at Holloway Prison in 2016 – just one example of cumulative injustices faced by black women at the hands of the British state.
SH   Whether it's Sarah Reed or Sandra Bland, it's about articulating a structural condition and it doesn't matter if it's 1919 or 2019. Both Korryn Gaines and Sandra Bland chronicled the threat of death that defines the lived experience of blackness. In vlogs and Facebook posts, they anticipated their deaths, understanding that any encounter with the state would place their lives in jeopardy. I think that their examples have failed to galvanise social movements in the ways that men's deaths have. Even in the context of something like Black Lives Matter, which was started by black women, you still need to start #SayHerName to make up for that gap of significance and regard. As we know, black women are as vulnerable to these forms of state violence, yet how do we underscore that? *Wayward Lives* closes with this figure – who is many figures – a woman hanging in her cell. The book is about the persistence and the tenacity of the everyday struggle to live, which dovetails with Sharpe's vision of 'wake work'. We live in the wake of these moments, they structure our existence but they don't blot out everything else. They don't exhaust everything else. The book describes the as if – as if we were free, as if a beautiful life were possible. It is earned by so much loss and destruction, blood and tears. It's not an easy celebration. It's not a vitalist rejoicing, but an extended meditation on the impossible and the necessary: *what does it mean to even imagine that life is possible* and to want something like the good life when life itself cannot be taken for granted; when one lives under the threat of death; when captivity is the prevailing scheme? How does one live in that context?

TWR   I was also reminded the phrase 'directed by desire', from June Jordan's poem 'When I or Else'. I saw it as a perfect descriptor for the women in *Wayward Lives*.
SH   Under capitalism there are so many forms of pleasure that are reproductive of the order. The forms of pleasure and joy and beauty that are also the focus here are those moments that are refusals and ruptures with the order. Again, the important question is: what does it mean to love that which can't be loved? What does it mean to even imagine, as a poor black girl, that you might have something like a beautiful life – one that's not about your self-annihilation, that's not about your conformity with norms or the meagre existence to which you

have been confined. That requires – is conditioned by – a certain refusal. It's to know yourself in the world you're a part of in radically different terms. For me that's the miracle of everyday survival.

TWR   What has been essential to your life as a writer?

SH   I feel fortunate because I have had such wonderful and brilliant teachers who have modelled so much, not only about how to write but about how to be a person of integrity in the world. I'm always thinking of my teachers. I also feel very lucky to be in the company of so many brilliant scholars of my generation. I'm constantly learning from my peers and that becomes food for me, it keeps me going. Music and quiet, those are things that are key to writing. I really do need more time to write, because when you're young there's a way that you can do whatever it takes – abuse yourself – to keep on writing, but I'm at this stage in life where I need to take better care of myself. Being a black woman in the world, I don't take living a long life for granted at all. So it's like *oh, how long do I have?* Do I have another decade of life? I don't know, I hope so.

TWR   Three final questions. 1) How do you define joy – what does joy mean to you? 2) What is your favourite colour? And lastly, a question you're asking yourself, or something you're telling yourself, from Saidiya to Saidiya.

SH   What is *joy?* What *is* joy? I tend to describe joy as this experience of transformation or release from the constraint or costume of the individual or the subject into this other form. So, for me I think it's about floating, it's about being nothing and being everything at the same time; this sense of the self disappearing in the context of the vastness of the earth, the ocean, the sky, the land. That kind of joy is always about self-dissolution, escape. And my favourite colour? My garden in full bloom. I'm a gardener, so I *love* the colours in my garden and I love just playing with colours. I'll show you my dahlias [shows image on phone], these are from my garden. Deep purples, deep burgundies towards black. The garden's blackest flowers.

 And finally, I don't know if I would have a question or advice, but probably the advice that I would give myself would be something like 'Don't despair'. *Don't despair.*

V.A.B.,
July 2019

JOHN O'REILLY

John O'Reilly's photomontages, which he began making in the 1960s, splice together images from gay porn magazines, art history and his own self-portraits. His erotic montages include fragments of works by Titian, Caravaggio and Velázquez, cut from books using a razor blade, combined with images of men in states of ecstasy – fucking, waiting to be fucked, or exhibiting their cocks for the camera.

The photomontages start as miniatures. O'Reilly creates dioramas in his studio, arranging the paper fragments on a wooden stage alongside miniature objects – plastic birds, toy soldiers or model ladders. He then photographs the scenes with a Polaroid camera, cutting up and splicing together these Polaroids to create seamless montages, which he touches up with a watercolour brush.

In his images, O'Reilly frequently makes tender, irreverent voyages into the studios of famous painters – Chardin, Bonnard, Picasso – inserting himself into their stories. In *Artist and Model* (1985), the first image shown here, a semi-naked O'Reilly plays the artist, appearing to sketch an angelic chiaroscuro youth ripped from a painting by Caravaggio. In *Around Amor* (1987), a found photograph of an atelier is transformed into a treasure trove of historical artefacts: a stack of lutes, the Elgin Marbles, Seurat's pointillist boy in a hat, vintage toys, a bent Madonna, and O'Reilly himself, naked on the floor. In his more recent work, O'Reilly has made paper montages, dispensing with the Polaroid entirely; in *Holding* (2018), a face from a Roman painting, with a long nose and sleepy eyes, morphs into a pair of buttocks held apart by stray hands, tacked on with masking tape.

At 89 years old, O'Reilly continues to exhibit internationally, most recently in the solo show 'A Studio Odyssey' at Worcester Art Museum (2017). His work first came to public attention in 1995, when it was featured in the Whitney Biennial. At the time O'Reilly was 65, living in Massachusetts and working as an art therapist at Worcester State Hospital for the mentally ill. Prior to this his erotic, art-historical fantasias were almost completely unknown.

PLATES

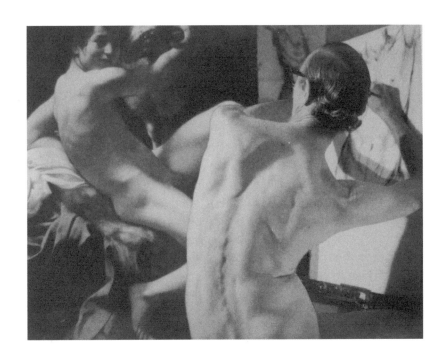

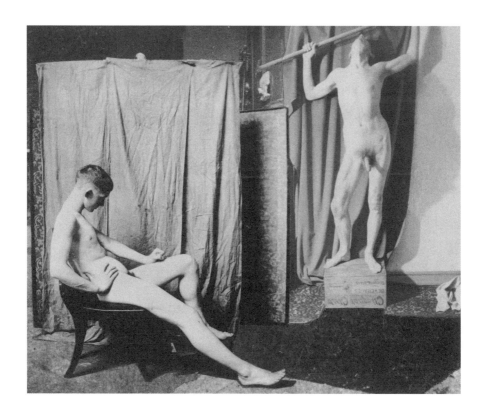

XXVIII

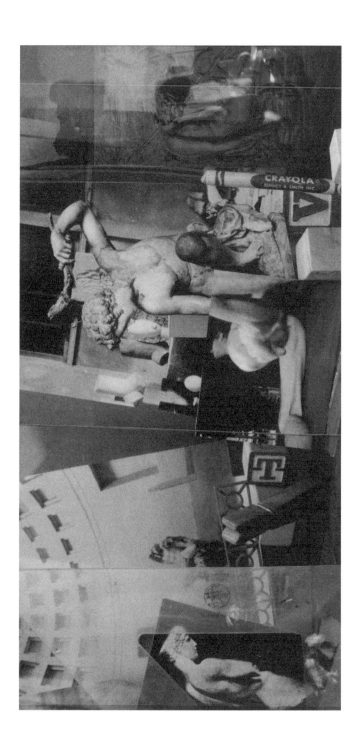

XXIX

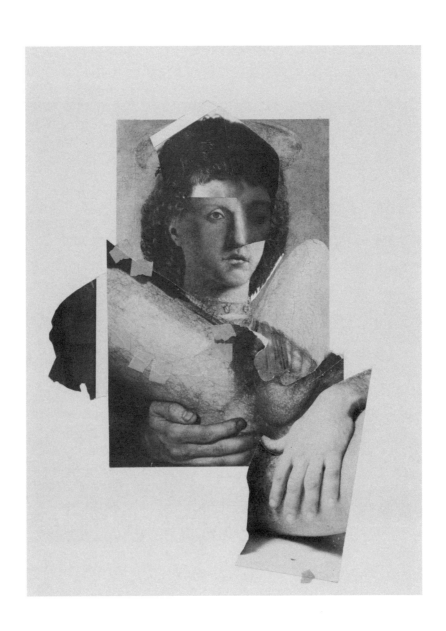

XXXVII

ALL CIRCLES VANISH
ANWEN CRAWFORD

Georges Franju's documentary *Le Sang des Bêtes* begins with the slaughter of a white horse.

A man leads the horse by its bridle through the gates of an abattoir. The horse and the man stand together in the courtyard of the abattoir.

The pressure applied by the man as he places a captive bolt gun to the head of the horse appears gentle, as the touch of one's lips upon the face of a person to whom you are saying goodbye, and perhaps for a long time.

I was young for a long time. Nobody died. Perhaps I wanted to die, or thought that I did, but that is not the same.

I don't know if the word *captive* in the phrase *captive bolt gun* refers to the bolt, held by pressurised air inside the gun barrel, or to the effect of the bolt upon an animal now held between living and death.

To be stunned. The word comes from *thunder.*

What I really mean is that no death had overturned me.

As the man drives the bolt through the brain of the white horse its legs buckle instantaneously. It seems to bounce from the pavement into the air before crashing onto its flank.

During the second semester of my first year at art school you bring a sequence of black-and-white photographs to class.

Our first year at art school. Some years after your death I find a notebook in which you have written MY WORK (in blunt pencil, as you always wrote), and then crossed out the MY for OUR. Our work.

I think of the way in which the horse turns its head in order to face the man who holds the captive bolt gun. Or the texture of the back of your hands and the ways in which you moved them.

I consider the sequence further, in my memory.

Your being warm.

Now I believe that the man pulls upon the horse's bridle.

The photographs you bring into class show you kneeling at night on a pavement, digging through the concrete till it cracks, and then planting a sapling in the new wound.

Sous les pavés, la plage!

That's when I know we have to be friends.

Your skin a little permanently browned; your panelled nylon zip-up jacket, also mostly brown, and mildly frayed; the rat's tail of red hair that ran past your shoulders, at least for a time, till you cut it off; your hands

The horse does not appear to anticipate what will happen when it turns, or is brought, to face the man.

Does the horse trust?

On my laptop I watch a contemporary police drama set in London featuring two women who are asylum seekers from Syria. Only it transpires that the women are not Syrian, they are Iraqi, and this fact of nationality makes them economic migrants, not asylum seekers, and so they are taken into detention. At the detention centre, a guard observes to a cop: *It's a lot like a slaughterhouse. You need to calm the animals.*

For an instant the horse with its forelegs drawn looks like the horse on a carousel.

The first thing we make together is a fence, unrolling the wire mesh across the width of the gallery / on Gadigal country.

Outside my window / on Bidjigal country a refrigerated truck pulls up and unloads its goods for the butcher.

The borders of present-day Iraq have existed only since the signing of the Treaty of Sèvres, in 1920, which allowed the victorious Allied Powers of the First World War to partition the Ottoman Empire between them. The Treaty of Sèvres was signed at the Sèvres national porcelain manufactory, in the suburbs of Paris.

Aux porte de Paris, reads the opening caption of *Le Sang des Bêtes*. At the gates of Paris.

August Macke, the German painter, was killed by French artillery fire on 26 September 1914, during the second month of the First World War. He was 27. His compatriot and fellow artist, Franz Marc, who had also been drafted, did not learn of August's death for nearly a month. *Oh dearest*, he wrote to his wife Maria, on 23 October, *the naked fact will not enter my head.*

At each end we staple-gun the mesh to the walls.

The horse isn't dead when it hits the ground. It is concussed, catastrophically.

In the succeeding shots the horse's bridle is removed and its throat is incised by another man, using a spike. The horse's blood makes a rush of steam as it spills from the warm interior of the body onto colder ground.

The year before we met I spent a week in the psychiatric ward, on suicide watch. In the interview room, the admitting doctor winced when I lifted my jumper, making visible the network of cuts across my torso.

You remove your shirt as we work – stupidly bare-handed! – to top the fence with barbed wire, and I watch you, surprised by your visible strength, and for a moment consider you in desire, but the moment passes and I never return to it.

Through the windows of the ward's common lounge I could see a billboard edging a nearby four-lane road; it read ESCAPE

A decade later you ~~would~~ die in the same hospital.

The development of the abattoir as a site beyond the boundaries of the city was motivated by a desire on the part of public health inspectors (among others) to remove unregulated private butcheries and slaughterhouses from heavily populated urban centres. It was believed that the visibility of animal slaughter had a morally corrupting effect upon the behaviour of the citizenry, young men in particular.

It felt like everyone was going crazy then; everyone around me, at least; everyone young. I was 18, turning 19. It was the first year of the new century.

It occurs to me that during the same year, you learnt that you had cystic fibrosis. This should have been diagnosed when you were a baby. At 19 you were adjusting to a truncated lifespan.

But what if I had died before we met? Or you had died?

I write *you* as if you are still alive to read this.

My housemate had a psychotic break. Friends phoned late, on the landline, self-harming and hazily suicidal. A hospital psychologist advised me to learn how to divorce my own moods from the state of the world.

In the spring, after the hospital, I went to Melbourne to protest against a meeting of the World Economic Forum / on Wurundjeri country. 20,000 people showed up, though the cops said half that number.

I look up the word *torso* and the dictionary says: *An unfinished or mutilated thing.*

If our natural curiosity hadn't been carefully repressed, we should quite naturally be very interested in what happens in slaughterhouses, and not need films like *Le Sang des Bêtes*

A temporary fence had been raised around the entire perimeter of Crown Casino, where the World Economic Forum was scheduled to hold its meeting over three days.

On the first day a comrade from Chile showed us a tactic they'd used during the years of the junta: you form a circle: it takes fewer people that way to block a space than it would to block the same with a straight line.

The carousel, or merry-go-round, has its origin in training games practised by Arabic horsemen during the time of the Crusades, from which the idea of circular jousting enters Europe.

It was the era of summit protests, as they were called. In 1999, major demonstrations had taken place in Seattle, outside a meeting of the World Trade Organisation. In 2001, 200,000 people would confront the G8, in Genoa.

Above my desk I keep a postcard reproduction of a photograph by Robert Mapplethorpe, *Two Men Dancing*, a gelatin silver print from a medium format negative. The two men – still so young, almost boys – are shirtless, perhaps naked (the image is cropped at their waists), and each wears a plastic crown.

Franju had a twin brother who fought in Algeria.

The summit protests were given binary nicknames after the month and date on which they began. Seattle was N30. Melbourne was S11.

It was 27 years to the day since the coup against Salvador Allende. We held hands and circled in the rain.

On 23 May 1871, during the Bloody Week that marked the suppression of the Paris Commune, the Tuileries Palace at the Place du Carrousel was burnt down by the Communards.

La barricade ferme la rue mais ouvre la voie

We must be a blancmange, said our Chilean comrade, *encircling the state.*

In front of the fence, when we have finished building it, we place two signs that we have stolen: REFUGE ISLAND and COMMONWEALTH PROPERTY, DO NOT TRESPASS

We name ourselves The Welcoming Committee.

On the second day the cops waited until past dark to break the picket lines. The media and their cameras had departed. We were rows deep facing off and watching them pull on their leather gloves, and I was frightened, but we held, arm to arm along the picket. The comrade next to me was wearing a leather jacket.

As the police chief says to Buñuel's Archibaldo de la Cruz: *If we arrested every-body who'd ever committed a crime in his imagination, there'd be more people in prison than out.*

immobilised, anaesthetised, suspended, and bled;

On the third day we danced to be rid of the night before – the pickets cleared by horses, blinkered and foaming, and cops climbing the fence from the inside and walloping people on the head.

Before we met, the year before, I dreamt of police horses; how a group of us were trapped inside a narrow house as the cops rode through and how they beat us with long-handled instruments.

For months afterwards we flinched at the sound of helicopters.

If his film had been in colour, said Franju, it would have been unbearable.

The Sydney Morning Herald, 19 April 1848, minutes of the Legislative Council

Mr LOWE presented a petition signed by 1,000 citizens of Sydney, praying that the council would take measures for the early removal of the various slaughterhouses from the city, and grant to the proprietors thereof such remuneration as might be adjudged reasonable.

The petition was read and received.

I went to art school thinking: *Start a band, change the world.* This was hopelessly outmoded.

I liked the idea of art school far more than the reality, but then, my idea was a bake of 'Common People' and what I'd read about the Bauhaus.

Der Blaue Reiter and associates, from left: Maria Marc, Franz Marc, Bernhard Koehler, Heinrich Campendonk, Thomas de Hartmann, Wassily Kandinsky.

I applied to art school because of pop music, more or less.

Owing most things in my life to pop music, including an indelible hatred of wage labour.

I was teenage in the Nineties and it felt like the answer was to die, but what was the question?

Something to do with shopping centres, something to do with microwaves,

The weekend after leaving the psych ward I went back to work; well, I had to pay the rent.

Bosnia, suburbia, band T-shirts, recuperation, Nokia mobile phones, ads at bus stops, export-processing zones. Have I told the joke about a friend who shelved Tony Blair's memoir in the True Crime section?

What was the question?

I dreamt I went to Woomera again. Dreamt when I was 17 of an arms dealer waving me behind a curtain and the dust and nausea has never left. Saw a colour plate of Franz Marc's painting in a book: *Tierschicksale*, The Fate of the Animals; I bring things together but the young stay dead / *stay beautiful*, we used to say. Now I want it to mean *dwell for a time / lightly / in time*, my friends.

Above my desk I keep a polaroid photograph of a silver-white-and-grey tabby kitten sat in the sunlight that falls through a screen door onto the boards of a hallway in the house / on Wangal country where I once lived. The house no longer exists.

Mounted police joined riot police on foot to force a passage through ————

Years after the fact I listen to two former members of the Tute Bianche discuss
the G8 protests in Genoa; the protests at which Carlo Giuliani was shot dead by
a member of the Carabinieri but the cops later said that the bullet was deflected
by a stone
into his body. The raids and the beatings. Enclosures. Additionally it seems that
the rebellion contained some idea that it was possible to rid the world of nobles.

Naturally, the dinosaur unions were there and I wasn't surprised to see school-
children ———————————————————————————————

————— highly organised ————————————————————

Force response officers stormed out of   Crown's Queensbridge

circles

in a baton charge.

If I invoke the ghosts of redressers past it is because I find myself afflicted by the sadness of thinking that it is too late to remember now the futures they were dreaming of including us dreaming of them, and not wanting to surrender to believing this, I picture myself hand in hand inside a loop of

evenings / the carlight / the sense there isn't time enough / to stumble / the cash machine / the glow in other people's / houses / the threshold

moving again
us moving
again moving
against

the violence of the state. I gather
I am gathered in the ghosts round.

       Do you

          dream me like I dream you impossibly
          real again. Lettrists, sisters. My echo   my
          spirits past the screen's mesh
          into the movement of the free. You and me
          in time there isn't time
          enough to stumble. We must fail
          everything failing too late to move fast
          each other again. Past the cash machine.

I didn't tell you that I'm aloud to go to some far distant places but not you.

seriously what about our plan to take over the world. don't think I've forgotten about it.

In front of the fence, when we have finished it, we place two signs that we have stolen: REFUGE ISLAND and COMMONWEALTH PROPERTY, DO NOT TRESPASS.

The white horse is dragged by its left hind leg inside the abattoir, where it is hoisted in chains, the better to enable its exsanguination.

I think we are in our first year when we go down to what would have been the holding cells for patients brought by boat along the Parramatta River to the hospital. Callan Park Hospital for the Insane was built according to the Kirkbride Plan, where the buildings' layout mimics a bat's wingspan.

Everything gets flattened and it is the nature of cities to be changed, but I realise now that we moved through the city at a time when some tattered things still remained in place: horse race tracks, flour mills, warehouses. These places kept a time, if not a purpose. We entered their time. You and me would just be hanging about and out of this will arise some ordinary adventure.

Pteropus poliocephalus, the grey-headed flying-fox,

From the dock, the patients were transported underground.

                                   which now more frequently
drop dead from the trees, overheated,

This would have been around the time of *Tampa*.

I press my hand to the sandstone.
                          nested in the trees around the art school,
once an asylum / on Gadigal country.

There must have been many days and evenings when we sat in the shed where you lived / on Gadigal country, or under the frangipani tree that I still think of as your tree, the metal chairs grown hot by the sun and beach towels bleaching in the branches, pink frangipani flowers, and yet what we might have said has left me.

Time before, and time before, and time remains and always more time and who is being here before and always, and what is done, and what was done, and what gets done, who holds the knife?

It might be that the first thing we make together isn't the fence inside the gallery but a fence outside of a gallery, in a courtyard of our art school.

I remember the photographs from *Tampa*: hundreds of people lying hot in the shadow cast by shipping containers stacked on deck, which were rust-red.

We paint the letter Q onto jumpers, string them up behind that fence. I don't remember this but it has been remembered to me.

We simply cannot allow ————————————————————————

        asylum seekers

irrespective of the circumstances, irrespective of ————————————
————————————————

———————————————————— stocking ————————

———————————————————————— density ——————

                  a sinking   boat

            the Taliban

    trying to sail to Christmas Island

——————————————————————————— the people —
————————————————

We don't turn ————————————

————————————————————————————————
————————— easy —————————

We climb into overlooked places.

People dismiss the time and space in between objects, you write, and I can feel your absence inside of your clothes I have been given now to handle.

The general meaning of *abattre* is: *to cause to fall* or *to bring down that which is standing.*

You build a walkway out of salvaged planks and it moves at jeopardising angles through a house that is afterwards demolished for a carpark.

excised offshore place means any of the following:

(a) the Territory of Christmas Island;

The development of the abattoir as a site beyond the boundaries of the city was instigated by Napoleonic decree on 9 February 1810. Five new locations for the slaughtering of livestock were chosen to replace nearly 400 private butcheries in Paris.

excision time, for an *excised offshore place*, means:

(a) for the Territory of Christmas Island—2 p.m. on 8 September 2001,

Then came the attacks on the World Trade Center.

Then the horse died. Then came the rendering machines.

It was 28 years to the day since the coup against Salvador Allende.

South China Morning Post, 11 November 1999

Senator Ross Lightfoot, of Western Australia, said illegal immigrants should be quarantined on the Christmas and Cocos islands, distant Australian territories in the Indian Ocean, a suggestion that horrified residents and outraged his parliamentary colleagues.

The senator, who is no stranger to controversy, said creating offshore colonies to house illegal immigrants would 'protect the mainland from disease'.

A new centre at Woomera in South Australia's north will open within two weeks.

Above my desk I keep a postcard made by a friend and it says *Another world is possible.*

I'll follow a street to its end for the promise implied by the way that the light falls.

I was teenage in the Nineties and it meant being too late for Cabaret Voltaire / the Cabaret Voltaire / Nanterre / Franklin River / Freedom Rides: all that was left was shopping centres, and rock stars swallowing their shotguns.

At hardware stores the salesmen address you and ignore me, assuming that I am the girlfriend. Lots of people make this assumption, which amuses us, and also goes to show that [Redstockings voice] *the hegemony of the couple form must be abolished!* I was teenage in the Nineties and I thought it meant that families, at least, were over.

But there were memories. An elderly gentleman, precisely dressed, gestured to the road that led out from Crown Casino and said: *Sitting on the tram tracks, now* that's *freedom*, and he meant it.

Sous les pavés, la plage!

Once we drive through the night / to Ngunnawal country to spend two days spray-painting an empty. Its windows are punctured. We navigate by candlelight. It's freezing in your car held together with whatever and we breathe in

rain / spray paint / you swim

What are you like? Once in a New York summer / on Lenape country (you are still alive, then) I am watching Chaplin's *The Gold Rush*; I seem to remember his cabin tipping into the lip of a crevasse, near to oblivion; the young boy sitting next to me laughs so hard he rises up out of his seat as his whole self shivers with laughter. What are you like? When I ride my bike from work shifts to art school and see you the day begins again.

I think of you when I see three sulphur-crested cockatoos wheeling a line across the sky. I think of you when the train lifts from a tunnel and the built world manifests again. I think of you ~~waking in~~ walking in the tunnels; I think of us in derelict houses, I think of the squats I could name but

We weren't too late for / with us or against us or
shop for / weapons or / deserts or / evidence

Franz, wrote Else Lasker-Schüler to her friend Franz Marc, *paint me a green sheep. There is nothing so outlandish left in the world, except me.*

We climb into overlooked places.

Men with brown names were arrested for saying or not saying and we said
how many times had we said
on the phone (*we?*)
bring down the government

The white horse is lowered to the ground, to be flayed. A man wearing a blood-
ied apron pumps compressed air in between the horse's flesh and hide. The white
fat below the skin is as enclosing as

This crusade, this —————————————————————

                  dread on a night when

————————————— *war on terrorism, is* ——————————

                           you wake from
being pressed into the hollow of

————————————————————— *going to take* ————

          a loss you cannot name

——————————————————————————— *a while.*

                   when you awake
from it.

*Australian ladies and gentlemen, We hope you accept regards and warm feelings of the
miserable and oppressed Afghan refugees turning around Christmas Island in the middle
of the sea,*

We must have met around this point, or maybe just before: September,

      while having no shelter,

                        your
sapling in the pavement and the way the water sings in the darkroom;

Of course, we are Australian.————————————————

your

laughter.

cloths to change after ten days and even toilet and
bathroom.

Asylum seekers rescued by the *Tampa* were forcibly transported by the Royal
Australian Navy to Nauru. The imprisonment of asylum seekers in island
detention centres funded by the Australian government would be known as the
Pacific Solution.

The word comes from the Latin, *solvere,* and retains its etymological root in the
meaning of *solution* as a form of loosening, generally in liquid, for instance:

William Dampier, the first white man to record a visit to Christmas Island,
owned a slave known as Prince Giolo, whose real name may have been Jeoly.
Prince Giolo was from Miangas, of the Talaud Islands, in the midst of the
Celebes Sea.

the

salt print, one of the earliest photographic processes, requires wetting paper
with a solution of sodium chloride in water. The paper is then dried.

The acronym SIEV, applied at this time by the government and military to asy-
lum seeker boats trying to reach Australia, has always struck me as being too
close to *sieve* for coincidence, hinting that the sea leaks people;

Jeoly was sold by Dampier for exhibition in London and Oxford.

moreover, *sieve*

as a verb suggests removal.

In London and in Oxford, what did he dream of?

Operation Enduring Freedom began on 7 October 2001, with British and United
States air strikes against Kabul, Jalalabad and Kandahar.

Which colour of sky? What bird calls?

When the bombing started did we protest outside the US Consulate / on
Gadigal country?

Why can't I recollect?

Wrote Franz Marc to Maria Marc on 14 March 1915, from the Western Front: *How is the woodpecker? Did the pair of red-tails come back?*

The movement of whose hands?

Did the pheasant come back?

But I dreamt I went to Woomera again. And sometimes I chase the edges of your presence upon waking.

My main thought now is:

Of course, we are Australian. ————————————————

                         the concept of a new world;

———————————————— We don't behave barbarically.

ISLE OF BATS, VERY LARGE; AND NUMEROUS TURTLE AND MANATEE
                                        always to create, to work for the future. *Kisses, Franz.*

The timing of the *Tampa* incident in the lead up to the 2001 federal election provided an opportunity for a hardline political response to unauthorised arrivals.

———————————————————————————— other SUNCs jumping overboard.

In subdued light a solution of silver nitrate is then brushed onto one side of the paper.

Some years after your death I am tasked with sorting out your negatives. I hold the lengths of film up to the sunlight / on Gadigal country: each frame a window on a past that will have happened.

The fact is the children were thrown into the water.

Which is not to say the photograph attests to a reality that has existed independent of the photograph.

No, well now you are questioning the veracity of what has been said. Those photos are produced as evidence ——————————————————————

The photograph only attests to the reality of time.

I am told ————————— it is an absolute fact, ————————— into the water.

The way the water sings in the darkroom, and making up the photograph from instruments of light and what we choose or will have chosen to leave out of the frame. The negative indexes the fullest set of possible solutions to the photograph that ends up being made, but the photograph will frame a truth only the photograph contains, apart from time, which goes on happening.

Our willingness to overlap.

There isn't one photograph of us, facing the camera.

          The threshold /

Due to its overcrowding ————————————————————————

                                moving again /

———————————— and need to maintain stability —————————

                                     us moving /

———————————————————— [the vessel] may be limited to a slow passage and —————————————

                                        again
moving /

——————————— therefore a later time of arrival—————————

        against / the violence of the state

————————————————————————— could be expected.

The earliest salt prints have ceased to exist, as they were made before a method to fix the image after exposure had been found.

Alya Satta,
Canti,
South Lampung Regency, Lampung,
Indonesia

July, 2019

Dear Alya,

I call myself into this space with you.

If you were alive as I write this, you would be 20.

I won't flatter myself by imagining that we would know each other, had you lived, or that anything could be redeemed by such a make-believe. I redeem nothing; not in words, not any way. You are dead and cannot read this. I write *you* as if you might read this.

What is this space? I imagine our movement through it as a falling without landing, and the space has always existed between us. I call myself into this space but I am always in this space, or will have been; I call myself to the attention of being in this space, which is is our differentiation, where I become me, and you you, and will have been, as me and you. And we have fallen together in our separateness that makes all possible; falling without landing through a space that always was, and is the space that makes a *we* possible, because there can be you and can be me.

That there was you. But there is no place now on this earth that contains you: you in yourself, irreducible and irreplaceable. In the space of our differentiation is no longer a place where we can meet, as you and me – though I have said I will not flatter myself by imagining this meeting, or this place. Perhaps just once, if you had lived, the train I will have been travelling on on a Saturday and yours will pass in opposite directions and a flash of bent heads as the carriages go by, and the pylons outside, the backs of houses, stubborn flowering weeds on the embankments. You would be 20 as I write this, had you lived. I was 20 then, when you were ~~boarding~~ being boarded on a boat. And now nearly 18 years have gone by since your death, and we have fallen together in our separateness, but when the other passes from this space—

Outside my window / on Bidjigal country, the winter sun announces itself along the awnings and my neighbours' roofs, palely. Fence, pale, wall, boundary wall, moat, ditch, trench. Enclose, cordon off, hem, pen, corral. I am told I learnt the names of colours, when I was as young as you. *Silver. Aquamarine.* These words exactly.

But Alya, can we think the colour without naming it? Does silver exist before *silver*? Clouds, rings, foil, dolphins: these exist, but could they be the colour in the absence of the word? And the word in which language? *Blaues Pferd.* I always thought that if a person could imagine a blue horse it meant a kind of freedom, not just whimsy — the freedom to imagine remaking a world that makes my peace by your death. I have been made by what was done, what has been done in my name, what I have made and I cannot redeem one part of this.

You would have laughed, at some time; in your young life you would have been laughing. And delighting in your mother's smell, and walking to her to be held and carried, and together you were *we. Silver* is فضي. *Blue* is أزرق.

Alya: I call myself into remembering that I have been always falling through this space with you, though you have passed from falling with me. There was a you and will have been me, and everything is possible and will remain so in the space that creates *we*, including the failure to remake a world where there is no place now that contains you.

ULRIKE ALMUT SANDIG
tr. KAREN LEEDER

not to be old and not to be young, but old
enough to be several things at once: Ulrike

and Almut, a great beast that walks upright
to be a strange beast, that can talk. amazed

at the beast that can say 'I', that can
remember. to be hungry like a beast, an

insatiable hunger for simple things like 'tree'
like 'father' and 'mother', like 'you' and 'me'

not to understand all kinds of things, but
to be old enough no longer to feel

ashamed. to be afraid of illnesses and
parents getting smaller, their laughter

in the alder behind the house like children.
to become lighter and lighter and blow

with the wind in any direction. to put down
roots in any town. to be a tree behind

mother and father's house. to have
no name, no longer to say: 'I am'

to be wood in a table, at which someone sits

nicht alt und nicht jung sein, aber alt genug sein
um mehrere Dinge auf einmal zu sein: Ulrike

und Almut, ein großes Tier mit aufrechtem Gang
ein seltsames Tier sein, das spricht. staunen

über das Tier, das ‹ich› sagen kann, das sich
erinnert. Hunger haben wie ein Tier, unersättlichen

Hunger nach schlichten Begriffen wie ‹Baum›
wie ‹Vater› und ‹Mutter›, wie ‹du› und ‹ich›

eine Menge von Dingen nicht begreifen, aber
alt genug sein, sich nicht mehr zu schämen

dafür. sich vor Krankheiten fürchten und vor
den kleiner werdenden Eltern, ihrem kindlichen

Lachen im Graswald hinter dem Haus. leichter
werden, leichter und mit dem Wind ziehen

in gleich welche Richtung. Wurzeln schlagen
in gleich welcher Stadt. Baum hinterm Haus

von Vater und Mutter zu sein. keinen Namen
mehr tragen, nicht länger zu sagen ‹ich bin›

Holz eines Tisches zu sein, an dem jemand sitzt

snow falls and disappears as it touches the ground
you breathe almost soundlessly. we are lying on the floor
of a northern sea under the weight of total darkness.
little sister, are you asleep? can you hear the pink noise
the roar of the ocean liners? the whales lose their way and drift
towards the brightly-lit shores. from here no constellations

in sight. nor from the bottom of the ocean and not
with your eyes closed, not at night, not when it snows, and never
in the orange glow of sky above the place you and I call
home. you breathe soundlessly. snow falls in chunks, in flakes
no, it falls apart. we are silent and drift side by side into
the trembling bottomless roar of this snow globe world.

Schnee fällt und verschwindet, sobald er am Boden aufschlägt
du atmest fast lautlos. wir liegen am Grund eines nördlichen
Meeres und halten dem Druck der völligen Dunkelheit stand
Schwesterlein, schläfst du? hörst du das rosafarbene Rauschen
der Überseeschiffe? die Wale verlieren an Richtung und treiben
an die beleuchteten Strände. von hier aus: keine Sternbilder

sichtbar. auch nicht vom Boden des Ozeans aus und nicht mit
geschlossenen Augen, bei Nacht nicht, nicht bei Schneefall, nie
am orange angestrahlten Himmel über deinem und meinem
Zuhause. du atmest lautlos. Schnee fällt in Brocken, in Flocken
nein, er zerfällt. wir schweigen und treiben nebeneinander in
diese schwankende, bodenlos rauschende Schneekugelwelt

whatever you do, don't say it with roses, don't say it
with flowers at all! snowball bush, camomile or

the frost flowers in my parents' cottage on the heath
they are all real. but we, you and me

are we not reality-proofed? say it
in fractals, say it in the stelliformity

of the Koch snowflakes on your coat
in winter, say it on an empty sheet

of paper folded into dragon curves. say it
for me in the sound of Peano curves, say it

for me in a piece for four hands, but don't make
a meal of it, man, instead be so kind

as to look past me those days when I
can't stand myself again. best would be

you don't say it to me at all. let it melt
on your tongue, slowly, this snowball

push it from side to side, I want to read it
from your lips like Mandelbrot, almond bread, fresh and warm.

sags bloß nicht mit Rosen, sags gar nicht
mit Blumen! Schneeball, Kamille oder

die Eisblumen im Heidehaus meiner Eltern
sind alle sind echt. aber wir, du und ich

sind wir nicht echtheitsgeprüft? sags
in Fraktalen, sags in aller Sternförmigkeit

der Koch-Flocken auf deinem Mantel
im Winter, sags auf einem unbedruckten

Papier, in Drachenkurven gefaltet. sags
mir im Klang der Peano-Kurven, sags

mir im vierhändigen Spiel, aber nimms
nicht so genau, Mann, schau lieber

gütig an mir vorbei, wenn ich mich schon
wieder nicht ausstehen kann. sags

mir am besten überhaupt nicht. lass es dir
Schneeball, auf der Zunge zergehen

schiebs hin und schiebs her, ich will es dir
vom Munde lesen wie Mandelbrot, frisch und warm.

.

I say everything twice,
do everything twice. I repeat

everything: every mistake
and every betrayal, always twice: TEST!

TEST! *I am a double-voiced song bird*
with a human face

and it's hard to see I'm an odd bird at all
when I sit in the fern tree

and double-clink, double-
click and creak

and grind with my beak. I am
a travel company luring

you South, as if happiness
really is buried below the equator.

but don't be deceived! I can't
be trusted, or if I can then

only twice. there's no helping
you, not even once.

I'm a little two-legged teapot
wearing my father's

black cassock, his white collar
and I carry with me

my mother's girlhood dreams.
when I leave you, it's

always twice:

once in the South, but just as a test
and once STOP! in the Northwest.

alles muss ich zweimal sagen, alles
muss ich zweimal tun. alles

muss ich wiederholen: alle Fehler
und jeden Verrat, immer zweimal: TEST

TEST! ich bin ein zweistimmig singender
Vogel mit Menschengesicht

und schwer als schräges Tier zu erkennen
wenn ich im Farnbaum sitze

und zweistimmig klirre, zweistimmig
klicker und mit dem Schnabel

knirsche und knarr. ich bin
eine Reisegesellschaft und lock dich

gen Süden, als läge das Glück
tatsächlich unterm Äquator begraben

aber lass dich nicht täuschen! mir
ist nicht zu trauen oder wenn

dann immer nur zweimal. dir
ist nicht zu helfen, kein einziges Mal

ich bin ein Teekesselchen auf zwei Beinen
und trage den schwarzen Talar

meines Vaters, seinen weißen Kragen
und die Mädchenträume meiner

Mutter trag ich auch mit mir herum
wenn ich dich verlasse, dann

immer zweimal:

einmal im Süden, aber das nur zum Test
und einmal STOPP! auf Nordwest

almost thirteen questions about Idomeni, 2016 AD

and what if love's not the answer after all?
and what if that dove doesn't go out and
fetch the first leaf it finds and bring it
back as a sign: land in sight? and what if
there's no clear daylight visible on the
waters ahead but instead just women and
children sinking? and what if there's not
a single jot of good *Deutsch* to be found
in this *Land* of mine but tarred and
feathered pity as a hyperlink, until I go
and forget my own language too? and
what are you up to? I'm drowning. I
don't mean that ironically either. my
conscience and me, we are rarely at one.
we find rhymes for our moral dismay
and do sweet FA. what is the right
question anyway? and what if Idomeni is
the only answer and a new way of
sinking between stools? do you trust me
or not, the Chancellor asked falling
between tables and waited for question
number nine: what makes for a plausible
case so that a man, a woman, a child are
not sent back home? I don't know right
from wrong. I'm talking about flailing in
icy water as a new form of sport. what
was the question again? and what if dove
weren't a brand that you can wash your
hands with and forget in all innocence?
coocoo, coocoo, Idomeni, there's blood
in the shoe. I wash my hands in the rain.

fast dreizehn Fragen über Idomeni, 2016 AD

und was, wenn love doch nicht die answer ist?
und was, wenn dove noch nicht das erste Blatt
vom Boden liest und wiederbringt als Zeichen:
Land in Sicht? und was, wenn überhaupt kein
klares Tageslicht auf den Gewässern sichtbar
ist, statt dessen lauter Männer, Frauen, Kinder,
die versinken? und was, wenn kein schöner
Deut in meinem Schland zu finden ist als
gefiedert und geteertes Mitleid zum Verlinken,
bis auch ich mein eigen Sprech vergessen tu?
und was machst du so? ich ertrinke. das ist
nicht sarkastisch gemeint. mein Gewissen und
ich, wir sind nur spartanisch vereint. wir
reimen Betroffenheitslyrik und rühren uns
nich. wie lautet die richtige Frage? und was,
wenn Idomeni die schlichte answer ist und
eine neue Art, zwischen die Stühle zu sinken?
vertraut ihr mir oder nicht, fragte die Kanzlerin
zwischen den Tischen zurück und wartete auf
Frage neun: wie lautet die glaubhafte Klage,
damit ein Mann, eine Frau, ein Kind nicht
wieder heimgeschickt wird? ich weiß nicht, was
richtig und falsch ist. ich spreche vom Wühlen
im unterkühlten Gewässer als einer neuen
Form von Bewegung. wie war noch die Frage?
und was, wenn dove doch keine Marke ist, die
man beim Waschen der Hände in Unschuld
vergisst? ruckedigu, Idomeni, Blut ist im
Schuh. ich wasch meine Hände im Regen.

AT THE HEART OF THINGS
VANESSA ONWUEMEZI

FICTION

there is no meaning. Hanging a picture on the wall I   give   a little too
much force to my thumb skin breaks under pressure an orb of blood   red   red
to dark red   to dry red   to skin   to iron   to rust   to heat   to sweat   to
yesterdays as we move, we move. Tuesday. Going into the city with the rest of
them sliding down the greased pole of means become ends. Let me tell you. I
slipped and travelled against the sharp grain of escalator, one flight of metal
before I hit flat floor and crack, to the back of my head. I cried like a child oh
I oh I said me   am in pain.

I was at work by the afternoon. At home by early evening feeling burning
scratches on the backs of my legs and the bruised curve of my head. My mind
curved bruised.

In bed, the sheets scraped and tugged me sore any way I tried to lie. I   face
down, looking for a cool place, stretched out an arm and all that was solid
dematerialised. I   a nothing slipped into water. Water, as pressure. I felt the
water as pressure. I'd always thought of pressure as a pushing down   oh   it
was every drop of water for miles working into me. There was nothing to my
fingers, no weight, no force on the pads of my feet, no cold draught wafting past
the hairs of my skin, no sound, no sight. I couldn't set my watch to nothing.

I waited. I couldn't scream, unaware of mouth or lungs to do so not
breathing, not dead, not alive. No fear. Not yet. Eyes wide open into dark,
and no sense. Unsayable.

The Friday, I dropped in on Uncle Padana. It was early summer: shadows
fold neatly round corners, light warms the backs of the hands until four and
cools before six. He answered the phone in a lady voice as I stood outside his
consulting room door, then buzzed me in, He's ready for you now. He was
sitting behind his desk, leaning back in his chair, looking boyish, expectant,
tired. A Ceropegia hung from the bookshelf and fondled the few hairs on his
head. As I moved into the room he stood and for me opened his arms.

I told him about the fall, the senseless black of that night. He cupped the
bowl of my head in his hands, throbbing sore into his palms.

'What painkillers you on?' he said. He speaks out of the side of his mouth –
gritted teeth, broke his jaw, never set right.

'Something weak,' I said.

'Do you feel weak, sick?'

I shook my head. 'Nothing,' cupped my elbow, rough pad, a graze dried red,
and the other elbow, the same.

'A crack to the head. Confusion, no doubt.' He took away his hands.

'Confusion isn't the feeling,' I said, 'and you were there, and cousin Rhumz
was there.'

'Was I kind?' Scratching a nail over the stubble above his lip.

'Kind?'

'Pleasant, agreeable.'

'You weren't there in your physicality, at least, too dark to tell.'

'No light to bounce off my face?'

'No light to see.'

'Black?'

'Deeper than black, than basalt, as deep as death. You were a presence, not yourself.'

'Well, take a light next time—'

'If there's a next time.'

'Yes, then I might know that I was kind to you.'

'You are.'

'I want to know if I am, truly.'

'You're serious?'

'Look around.'

I looked. A yellow corduroy sofa. The long list of clients whose arses had worn it down talking it out for the cure, a long stack of them stretching up to the crows. To the left, a wall of books. The wooden floor, with a walking path where varnish was worn to the wood. Piles of paper. Three pairs of glasses. The room was a rectangle. That plant was the only plant. Us three the only living things in the room that I could see. The things I could not see: mice beneath the floorboards, dust mites, woodlice work their way into gaps come out at night. A window. Outside, a high wall, over which street life ran along as water runs downstream.

'I'm all about your night visits. You tell me, you tell me everything.'

'Okay.' I hugged him.

'Rest your head dear, lie horizontal. I worry.'

'I will.' I was out of the room.

'Call your sister?' he said, as the door closed behind me.

We were eleven when our father died. Sunday morning and I reached for my phone, touched her name and let it ring, no answer, but I felt she was at the other end watching it ring. A petty satisfaction I had then I was petty, pleased because she was so petty. Our blood was separated at birth but still runs hot through both of us. There was no big feud, that would be too easy, simply, we both need the upper hand. Our father died   he died. Twenty years of hot friction had passed since then. He cooled the blood. He waved the flag to signal the end of the race. He's dead. We found no way of being without him.

That night, I took the bedside lamp, an arm outstretched from the sheets. Light in my hand to extend my gaze solid shield against darkness. My hand backlit glowing. I pointed the lamp downwards, illuminating my feet, thighs, chest, arms, all there. It was snowing. I watched it fall through the lamp beam. Then I was afraid, and the cuts on my legs did burn then. The light would only penetrate a metre in any direction, and beyond that a void contained me. Last time I was there I was a nothing, now, myself and body entirely oh   I shone light in a circle around while the white stuff fell into darkness beneath me. Arm moving against dense water, resisting. I   floating   an obstacle in

the snow's path. It settled into the hollows of my collarbones and attached
to ragged braids of hair, but I couldn't feel it. It weighed nothing.

I wrote everything down after then: the pressure, I'm becoming accus-
tomed; time undeterminable; snowfall, grey-white, like pieces of bleached
moss; sense presence of Padana like hands cupping my head, Rhumz a tickling
at the top of my throat and eyelids, as if singing a high note; no sighting of
a living thing   yet   no skin and bone other than mine yet.

Some research at The Gross Library. I looked for oceanography and geol-
ogy, cruised the pages of *The Silent World*, *The Deep*. I'd travelled deep under-
water, so deep I knew that. My cousin, Rhumz, had been the librarian at The
Gross for years, until she had the kids. I'd catch her in the toilets sometimes,
brushing her tongue in front of the mirror. My habit of going to The Gross
stayed after she left. I sat at library desk with head propped on my hand let my
thoughts run through into evening. Looking out of the window, a streetlight,
a fox inside the light's yellow triangle, looking up, tipping back its head, black
tipped ears folding back, dipped ink black, catching yellow falling from the
streetlight. Then gone.

At home, I picked up the phone. I said, 'You were with me last night,
Rhumz.'

She said, 'Ha, sweetheart. Where was I last night? (Voice quieted as she
turned to bring in her husband.) I was cleaning some five-year-old-child gunk
out of the U-bend wasn't I?'

'Yeh,' he said.

'What else will they find for their fun and games? The dangers of children,
the perils of living with children. It's us who need protecting cousin, it's us
who are naïve cousin. How could I have been with you?'

I said the same thing that I said to Padana, though Rhumz was a different
temperament, a different grain.

'Presence? Well fuck me, I've always wished I could be two places at once.
But I never was there, not me. You know one of them left a little nugget of
something at my front door, on the mat. They think they're all cats and dogs
and little elf people. The kids think they can be anything they want. Leaving
little shits over the mat. I'm a cat or a dog they say, and that works for them.
Cousin, don't let them fool you, the perils of family life it's too late for me.
The party's over after a point. It's all old cigar stubs from then on. How's your
sister?'

After Rhumz, I called sister again. Again, no answer. Had I finally turned
her off? There were only a few axes of love, hate, attention in this world to
sustain me, Padana, Rhumz and Sister – Grindy. She was where? I never got
very close to her. Voice at the end of the phone, sometimes. Voice from across
the table. Face at the other side of a grave. Wet eyes returning my gaze. I'd
always fancied that her back was covered in acne, warts, moles with roots deep
into the heart of her.

A fantasy close to me at this point. I small as a flea scaling her back, looking for a foothold such as a protruding mole, ingrown hair, pimple. I reach the base of her neck, she screws her head around to look at me and I fall I scream so deep it pains my chest   pain I was falling.

I poured a glass of vodka, warm, and paced. As I passed the bookcase a spike of pain. A small shard of glass lodged in my foot, a fresh wound to join the others. I washed it with some drink, dabbed it with a tissue and drank more and sat down one minute and the next, I was in the snow. My lamp, shining right at me, suspended about a metre in front, glass in my hand.

The snow was dead matter, faecal matter and inorganic matter. Over weeks it falls from the ocean's surface to the deepest layers. A tug at my foot. Sharp teeth, a tail, something that liked my blood. The first time feeling something here. Oh   I felt the teeth sharp in me and I liked the feel. I'll say it again I liked it. The pink eel rasped at my foot, coiling itself and flexing, tugging, eyes black as the surround. I flicked my foot and it held on, my heel fresh meat to chew, so I kicked downward harder and it let go. I followed it with my lamp beam as it undulated, body S-shaped light and shadow. I moved as if running, fanning my arms out behind me   downwards   downwards into the dread, now only the eel I had for company. And, Padana and Rhumz I sensed in the dark.

The eel led me to a pool, I examined it piece by piece. A blue lagoon encrusted at its edges with smooth, charcoal-black pebbles, a slick mist of ochre hung above it. The eel disappeared into it and never reappeared into my light. Water beneath water? Dead crabs and eels lined its edges. The black pebbles, at a closer look, were mussels, mouths open, ready to swallow me oh   terrifying and so   beautiful it has to be seen unsayable beyond I know. I put my feet onto its surface and felt it push back. Wisp of blood from my heel drift away. To feel my feet. I didn't have feet before they had something to stand on. A Surface. Now my feet were accustomed. Unsteady though   it was   unsteady the surface could have swallowed me.

A red light. Legs kicked I held the lamp with one hand, plug dipping into the lagoon. I followed the red light, just like the eel moved, undulating my legs as if they were swinging ropes and I drifted forwards so slowly at first it took time. But there was so much time. I'm getting used to it. Approaching the red light, I pointed the lamp. Teeth transparent pincers, eyes glancing to its sides – foil dishes, as its dagger head cut through dark water. It travelled without fear, it had a red light beneath each eye, for lighting the way? That hinged mouth. It didn't hurry away from me. I followed and forgot for how far or how long we burrowed into dark, me and this fish. A long swim through the deepest layers. Long swim through the snow into the nothing beyond sight lines overhead. And pool after pool, haze beneath my feet. Overhead there were bioluminescent pathways. And mine, my lamp beam, my red light fish.

I followed the fish into morning. My vodka had spilled into my lap. Head jerked back over the sofa arm, dried spit on my chin. My foot was red, dried blood, the glass was cutting not so deep. But the memories of the glass, deep buried like a weight, my heart of lead. He had been sitting here one night, though I had taken back his key. He'd been sitting here naked one night. Light on he stood, dry skin, looked scratched and sore, limp penis, which he put in my hand. Limp like a soaked cloth. It was I who'd limped him, he'd said. I held the penis in my hand. In part because it was warm and my hands were cold and shaking. For old times' sake   then. The glass was thrown later. In the struggle.   The glass was thrown to give me time to run away. To give me time to run and to find the edge. I changed the locks after a few   days.

Malacosteus niger. The fish can be found in the midnight zone, with a flashing red cheek for attracting prey. Though its nature not as violent as its teeth. It was an ugly companion, led me further than I'd have dared to go alone with just the lamp light. *Synaphobranchidae*, the eel that ragged my foot for the taste of blood. The lake was filled with brine, a cold seep, salt deposits from sea after sea, leaching out from below the bed. The ochre haze of bacteria floating above it thick cloud of cells a soup wants to be left alone undisturbed, I know I understand. I knew its surface and the sense of my feet.

Leaving the library that night. I walked down the fox's alleyway, past that lonely streetlight, fried chicken bones. Once out of its beam I waded through that pink city darkness. As I walked along dark alley black shoes dipped into tarmac. Legs swinging black. Feet kick through black. Only I could really know what I'd seen. I spoke with Uncle Padana about the visits, as he'd asked. I'd hear his pencil burning at the other end of the line he'd go quiet, cooking up diagnoses feebly but in true he was stumped. I called Sister again a few times, again and nothing. Thick air between us.

I should have known that she would show up the next time. Unlike the others she was there in the flesh. Unlike me, she looked dead. Her skin yellow, as always, but pale, above us a ceiling of flashing fish cruised along. Her hair in thick bulging soft braids which wafted around her face, obscuring, reappearing and she was silent. She was dressed the same as me. She always dressed same as me that was something I hated about her. Hated her ability to dress. The only difference was that she was wearing shoes, black front buckle. I moved closer to my sister. Her feet and hands were puckered. My face inches from hers, her eyes were open staring ahead into the lamp, brown irises illuminated. Then she blinked, slow. Mouth opened and closed, mechanical, like a young bird begging for food. The eyes moving but no fixed gaze. Her limbs and head only floated, drifting with the currents. I moved to touch her, but I couldn't. My hand a weight, her puckered feet in my eye line. I was alone. I swivelled my lamp about me, I was close to the bed. Tube worms, red lipped, floral, spread like grass beneath me there was no room for standing.

I've seen an eel tie itself into knots, poisoned by the brine. I'd shone my light on it. Grindy's eyes had seemed empty as the eel's. She was retreated deep inside, so deep her body was just another floating debris fallen from the surface, her eyes opaque as the brine pool. The eel's head had jerked back and forth – the crack of a whip. It was momentarily surrendered to a powerful terror. Soul a black seed underwater. But it did survive.

After then, my travels down the tube rails seemed the stranger thing. Travelling into the city with the rest of them, sliding down the   Eye contact eyes snap away. The city demands a certain kind of contact only. It demands suspicions. Changes the meaning of a glance or a look of love, to yourself you keep your looks only to your own chest. It begins with everybody and nobody. People   flashing lights they   shoes, make-up, rats tails and so on   hinge necked bulb headed   bug eyed. We are all alike in this strangeness. But
I was accustomed to the dark pressures of the water oh   I'm no longer accustomed to this.

Last time. I found myself at the edge of a trench. At the edge, lamp in hand. Trying to see into it there was no point. Legs kick into black. I shone my lamp over the edge, but the light was swallowed. No point in the lamp light, too deep. I turned, they were all there. Everywhere I shot a beam there was Padana, Rhumz with Husband, the kids, getting on with things: moving rocks, feeding the tube worms, corralling the few fish into neat groups according to size, colour and temperament. And I was grateful but I had to go.

I circled around them, a farewell lap, handed Uncle Padana my lamp, kicked past the brine pools and the spiked rocks and dead eels, mussels. No point in the lamplight, too deep. No point in eyes too deep. No point in explaining. No way of making sense of

'Ta-ta.'

I tossed my chin over my shoulder and waved as I went over the edge. If I could pass on something, it would be to say that at the heart   at the heart at the heart of things there is no sense. Sister. I brushed the tips of my fingers on the ledge of the seabed as they

waved me off.

NUAR ALSADIR is a poet, essayist and psychoanalyst. She is the author of the poetry collections *Fourth Person Singular*, a finalist for the 2017 National Book Critics Circle Award for Poetry and shortlisted for the 2017 Forward Prize for Best Collection, and *More Shadow Than Bird*. She is a fellow at the New York Institute for the Humanities and works as a psychotherapist and psychoanalyst in private practice in New York. 'Morphine' is modified from her talk in Faber's Literature & Psychoanalysis series, delivered at Bloomsbury House in London on 8 April 2019.

KHAIRANI BAROKKA is an Indonesian writer and artist in London, whose work has been presented extensively, in fifteen countries. She is a PhD by practice researcher in Goldsmiths's Visual Cultures Department, and is currently Modern Poetry in Translation's Inaugural Poet-In-Residence. She was an NYU Tisch Departmental Fellow and is a UNFPA Indonesian Young Leader Driving Social Change for arts practice and research. She is co-editor of *Stairs and Whispers: D/deaf and Disabled Poets Write Back* (Nine Arches), author-illustrator of *Indigenous Species* (Tilted Axis; Vietnamese translation published by AJAR Press), and author of the debut poetry collection *Rope* (Nine Arches Press). Her work has been published in *The New Inquiry*, *Poetry Review*, *Asymptote*, *The Rialto*, *Ambit*, *Magma*, and other journals, anthologies and art books. *Selected Annahs* is part of a book in progress.

SUBHASHREE BEEMAN is an artist and translator from French, Spanish and Tamil. She has a Master's in Translation from The Open University, UK. She lives in Eden Prairie, Minnesota.

VICTORIA ADUKWEI BULLEY is a poet, writer and filmmaker. She is the winner of an Eric Gregory Award, and has held artistic residencies internationally in the US, Brazil, and at the V&A Museum in London.

SOPHIE COLLINS grew up in Bergen, North Holland, and now lives in Glasgow. She is the author of *Who Is Mary Sue?* (Faber, 2018) and *small white monkeys* (Book Works, 2017), a text on self-expression, self-help and shame. Her translation of Lieke Marsman, *The Following Scan Will Last Five Minutes* (Pavilion, 2019), was published earlier this year. She is a lecturer at the University of Glasgow.

ANWEN CRAWFORD is an Australian writer, critic and visual artist. This is an extract from a manuscript in progress, to be published in Australia in 2020 by Giramondo.

SARAH FLETCHER's second pamphlet *Typhoid August* was published by Poetry Business in 2018 as part of the New Poets Prize. Her poetry has been published in *The Rialto*, *Poetry London* and *The London Magazine*, among other places, and she was a Foyle Young Poet of the Year in 2012. She is currently working on a long poem titled 'PLUS ULTRA'.

ELAD LASSRY was born in Tel Aviv and he lives and works in Los Angeles. He has exhibited internationally including solo shows at frac île-de-france, Paris (2019); Sommer Contemporary Art, Tel Aviv (2019); 303 Gallery, New York (2019); Vancouver Art Gallery (2017); Kunstnernes Hus, Oslo (2012); White Cube, London (2011); and Kunsthalle Zurich (2010). Group exhibitions include Walker Art Center, Minneapolis (2016); The Museum of Modern Art, New York (2014); Turner Contemporary, Margate (2013); 54th Venice Biennale (2011); and The Photographers' Gallery, London (2011). A forthcoming exhibition at San Francisco Museum of Modern Art (SFMOMA) opens in January 2020.

KAREN LEEDER is a writer, translator and academic, and teaches German at New College, Oxford. She translates a number of German writers into English. She was awarded an English PEN award and an American PEN/Heim award for translations from Ulrike Almut Sandig's *Dickicht* (2011) which appeared as *Thick of it* (Seagull, 2018). Her translations of Sandig's poem cycle *Grimm* appeared as a limited edition pamphlet with Hurst Street Press in 2018.

JULIANA DELGADO LOPERA is an award-winning Colombian writer and historian based in San Francisco. She is the author of *Quiéreme* and the bilingual oral history collection *¡Cuéntamelo!*, which won a 2018 Lambda Literary Award. *Fiebre Tropical* won the 2014 Joseph Henry Jackson Literary Award from the San Francisco Foundation.

GBOYEGA ODUBANJO is a British-Nigerian poet born and raised in East London. He is a Roundhouse Resident Artist and his debut pamphlet, *While I Yet Live*, was published by Bad Betty Press in 2019.

VANESSA ONWUEMEZI is a writer and poet living in London. She graduated from the MA Creative Writing course at Birkbeck in 2018. 'At the Heart of Things' won the White Review Short Story Prize 2019.

JOHN O'REILLY is an artist born in Orange, New Jersey in 1930. He received his BFA from Syracuse University and MFA from the School of the Arts Institute of Chicago. O'Reilly has lived most of his life in Massachusetts hermetically developing his visual language, sharing his work largely with close friends. His momentous public discovery came when his work was included in the 1995 Whitney Biennial at age 65. His work is in the collections of the Museum of Modern Art, New York, the San Francisco Museum of Modern Art, the Museum of Fine Art Boston and the Addison Gallery of American Art, Andover. Now aged 89, O'Reilly continues to collage and exhibit his work across the country.

ULRIKE ALMUT SANDIG was born in East Germany and lives in Berlin with her family. Two books of stories and four volumes of her poetry have been published to date, including most recently, *Ich bin ein Feld voller Raps verstecke die Rehe und leuchte wie dreizehn Ölgemälde übereinandergelegt* (2016). She frequently collaborates with film-makers, sound artists and musicians and her CD with her poetry band LANDSCHAFT appeared in 2018. Sandig has won many prizes, including the Leonce and Lena Prize (2009), the Literary Prize of the Federation of German Industries (2017), the Wilhelm Lehmann Prize (2018) and the Horst-Bingel Prize (2018).

IZABELLA SCOTT is an editor at *The White Review*.

SHUMONA SINHA is a French author, born in Calcutta in 1973, who has lived in France since 2001. Her harsh but multilayered poetical literary reckoning with France's asylum system, *Assommons les pauvres!* (Editions de l'Olivier, 2011), from which her piece in this issue is extracted, made her famous overnight. She has received the Valéry Larbaud award, the Eugène Dabit Populist novel award, the Internationaler Literaturpreis HKW in Berlin, and was shortlisted for the Renaudot Award. The novel has been adapted by four theatres in Germany and Austria. Her third novel, *Calcutta*, has been rewarded, among others, by the French Academy (2014) for her contribution to the French language and literature. Translated into German, Italian, Hungarian and Arabic, Shumona Sinha's books are part of scholarly programmes at universities in France and the USA. She has a M.Phil degree in French linguistics and literature from the Sorbonne University, and taught English and French in high schools in the Parisian region for 14 years.

HANNAH QUINLAN AND ROSIE HASTINGS's practice explores the politics, histories and aesthetics of queer space, through video, performance, drawing and installation, in an increasingly difficult cultural landscape amidst the closure of queer venues, austerity and the buying-out of community spaces in the UK. Recent exhibitions and commissions include: 'Kiss My Genders', Hayward Gallery, London, 'Move Festival', Pompidou Centre, Paris, 'Queer Spaces', Whitechapel Gallery, London and Art Night, London, all 2019. The artists will present their first institutional solo exhibition at Focal Point Gallery, Southend in February 2020.

PLATES

Axiomatic by Maria Tumarkin is published by Fitzcarraldo Editions on 1 November 2019.

'Maria Tumarkin's shape-shifting *Axiomatic* deploys all the resources of narrative, reportage and essay. It is a work of great power and beauty.'
—— Pankaj Mishra, *Guardian*

Fitzcarraldo Editions

Middlesbrough Institute of Modern Art has a civic agenda to put art into action. We connect art, people and ideas. We work with communities to address current issues within politics, economics and culture. Our programmes encompass urgent themes such as climate change, migration, inequality, ageing and wellbeing.

We offer changing exhibitions, collection displays, learning activities, projects and community-focused initiatives that involve many artists and publics. These programmes promote creativity for everyone in ordinary life, through education, debate and making.

@mimauseful
mima.art

PLYMOUTH COLLEGE of ART

FREE ENTRY
SAT 7 - THU 12 SEP

Plymouth College of Art Postgraduate Centre is home to an active, cross-disciplinary community of makers and thinkers, whose work emerges from a dialogue between art, craft and design disciplines.

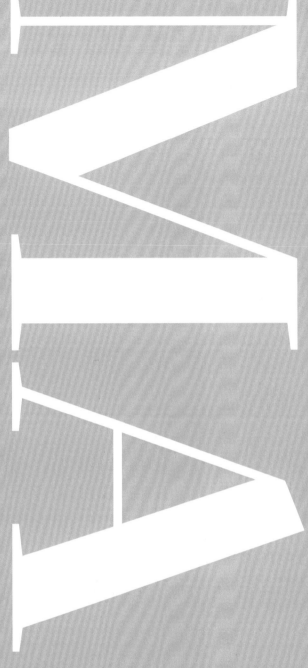

Places still available for our 2019 MA programmes. Email **liaison@pca.ac.uk** to book a visit or to chat to our MA tutors.

Postgraduate Centre, 44 Regent Street, PL4 8BB

plymouthart.ac.uk

'I work to earth my heart'

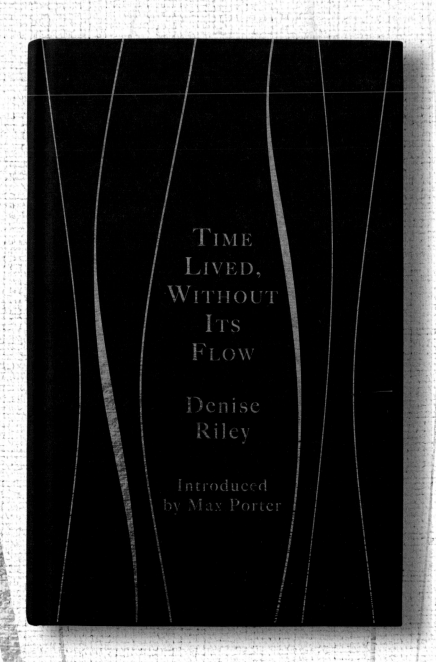

The remarkable, unflinching essay on the nature of grief
and time by critically acclaimed poet Denise Riley.

03 OCTOBER 2019

PICADOR